# ENTREVOIR

CHRIS KATSAROPOULOS

LUMINIS BOOKS

LUMINIS BOOKS
Published by Luminis Books
1950 East Greyhound Pass, #18, PMB 280
Carmel, Indiana, 46033, U.S.A.
Copyright © Chris Katsaropoulos, 2015

Cover art and design by Brit Godish.

Hardcover ISBN: 978-1-941311-49-3
Paperback ISBN: 978-1-941311-50-9

Printed in the United States of America

10 9 8 7 6 5 4 3 2 1

# LUMINIS BOOKS

*Meaningful Books That Entertain*

# Praise for *Antiphony*:

"What I found most engaging about *Antiphony* are the questions it raises . . . The story is fascinating, and the writing is powerful and poetic."

—Joseph Yurt, *Seattle Post Intelligencer*

"*Antiphony* is a book so eloquent and brilliant that it requires time—that precious entity few seem to have saved for exploration of the arts—to explore this obvious treasure. It is related to the great works of literature—James Joyce, T.S. Eliot, Virginia Woolf, Solzhenitsyn, Dante Alighieri, Roberto Bolaño, Tolstoy, Proust, Kazantzakis, Kafka, Melville, and Conrad."

"Katsaropoulos' grasp of physics is astonishing as is his ability to phrase theory in a manner comfortably decipherable. His deep entrenchment in literature and in music blossoms on the pages frequently. His grasp of the manifold variations of human relationships breathes of psychology breeding with philosophy. But most of all it is the serene beauty of his writing that mesmerizes and results in starting the book again once finished that proves this is a man of letters who has an enormous gift and future."

— Grady Harp, poet—*War Songs;* critic—*Literary Aficionado;* art historian—*The Art of Man, Vitruvian Lens* and *PoetsArtists;* writer for art museum catalogues.

"Hold on to your chair or you will be totally transported out of your comfort zone by *Antiphony*. It doesn't matter if you haven't the foggiest idea what String Theory is. . . What does matter is that you will fall down a metaphorical rabbit hole alongside a scientist driven to prove his theory. Katsaropoulos is an emerging fresh literary voice not to be overlooked."

—Rita Kohn, *NUVO Newsweekly*

"*Antiphony* is, in many ways, an awe-inspiring novel. It was, I think, written in awe. Awe of science and reason. Awe of intuition and faith. Awe of the one and the many . . . Katsaropoulos has a way of delving deeply into what seem like small moments and capturing all their nuances and vibrating tension."

"It makes me wonder how he did it."

—Al Riske, *Thoughts with Nowhere Else to Go*, author of *Precarious* and *Sabrina's Window*

"I enjoyed this book a lot. *Antiphony* is super smart but also accessible. It delves deeply into scientific theory as well as philosophy and some psychology but uses layperson language and felt really accessible to me."

"The writing style reminds me of Milan Kundera. I'm a huge fan of Kundera's work… so this is a big compliment. I think Kundera has a really unique voice and style that I never see anywhere and Katsaropoulos has a similar quality that lent some magic to the reading for me. *Antiphony* blends reality and non-reality in a fabulous way."

—Kathryn Vercillo, *Diary of a Smart Chick*

# Praise for *Fragile*:

"*Fragile* is a beautifully-written novel . . . the writing is uniquely refreshing. After reading *Fragile*, I found myself feeling very contemplative. Readers will enjoy *Fragile* and will find meaning in it that applies to their own lives . . . Highly recommended."

—Paige Lovitt, *Reader Views*

"Mesmerizing and beautiful, a truly stunning book! Katsaropoulos' first novel sets the bar incredibly high. In what can only be described as a truly unique style, the author takes us from the thoughts of one character directly into the next: an ongoing narrative of a brief portion of these three lives, to a moment of intersection so hauntingly profound and exquisite, it will leave the reader astounded and deeply moved."

"With a debut such as this, I see a wonderfully promising future for this author. A story and characters you will never forget, with a message as old and true as time itself. I have already read this twice, and marveled at it even more the second reading. I cannot recommend this book highly enough! A true classic for the ages."

—Lauri Coats, *ReviewTheBook.com*

"There is an element of higher meaning in this story that makes it fascinating to finish and to contemplate the experience of reading it. For lovers of experimental literature, this book is tasty."

— Grady Harp, poet—*War Songs;* critic—*Literary Aficionado;* art historian—*The Art of Man, Vitruvian Lens* and *PoetsArtists;* writer for art museum catalogues.

# Praise for *Complex Knowing*:

"These abstract, interpersonal poems buck form and embrace contrast. Traditional syntax and line breaks are abandoned for a richly poetic tone, and in this manner, Katsaropoulos hits all of the big themes: the archetypal, the idiosyncratic, and the fragile. The many shades of meaning and great depth of perspective are rewarding. Just shy of fifty short poems, this book digs deep… Katsaropoulos' collection is a poignant and necessary delivery of the most wonderful of human capacities, our ability to withstand the hurt and the joy."

— *Booklist*

"Chris Katsaropoulos' mind is so attuned to poetry, classical music, metaphysics, physics, science in general and man's search for meaning that his poems have passages, not unlike cadenzas in a piano concerto where the artist takes a pause from the orchestral score to expound on a note or phrase or thought that shows muscular and spiritual dexterity before returning to the work as a whole, that sing like few other poets can write."

"It is this gift that Katsaropoulos displays in this masterful work. One of the ways he accomplishes this is his apparent disdain for the confines of phrasing or punctuation or the manner in which he places his poems on the page: once the reader takes the time to read the poems aloud, the myriad levels of meaning surface—levels influenced by the life circumstances and experiences the reader brings to the poem. He writes as though a passing word or phrase or thought draws him to pen and paper and from that initial seed his imagination and stream of conscious sensitivity weave extraordinary images."

"He allows a certain ambiguity of thought that opens a passage for the reader to enter the creative process, introducing here and there phrases that may be read with several levels of meaning. Gently tucked into his poems are moments of strangely chosen rhyming words that adds to the mystery of the fluidity of what he is expressing. Make no mistake: once his individual poem is completed the thought process is there: it is the discovery of the process, that idea, that sixth sense place that is the joy of reading his work."

"This is a collection of fragments not unlike the encounters we all face in life—moments that seem coincidental and unimportant at the time but which later lead to insights and even behavior changes completely unexpected."

"*Complex Knowing* is most assuredly one of the more important collections of poetry by an American writer to come before the public. And as much as his novels continue to be unique contributions to literature, we can only hope that he will pause frequently to offers poems such as these."

— Grady Harp, poet—*War Songs;* critic—*Literary Aficionado;* art historian—*The Art of Man, Vitruvian Lens* and *PoetsArtists;* writer for art museum catalogues.

"The poems in *Complex Knowing* are illusive but very human, accessible and complex, cosmic and archetypal, a study in contrasts. Taking the time to understand them is the Rosetta Stone for this collection, and the reader who searches will find a wealth of meaning and enjoyment."

—*Examiner*

*Also by* Chris Katsaropoulos:

Novels

*Fragile*
*Antiphony*
*Unilateral*

Poetry

*Complex Knowing*

# ENTREVOIR

*I saw the mystic vision flow*
*And live in men and woods and streams,*
*Until I could no longer know*
*The stream of life from my own dreams.*
—George William Russell, Æ

*But we all, with unveiled face beholding as in a mirror the glory of the Lord,*
*are transformed into the same image from glory to glory, even as from the*
*Lord the Spirit.*
—II Corinthians, 3:18

"YOU CHOSE THIS LIFE," she is saying, her dark eyes staring back at him like two placid obsidian mirrors. "You wanted to come here." Jacob considers the implications of this and finds there is nothing he can say in his own defense. In that way she has of disarming him with ultimate reality, her attacks have always benefited from the casual elegance of an Asian martial artist, leveraging his own misguided words or deeds into the momentum that serves to bring him crashing down to earth.

The most he can do is offer an explanation, which is not the same as an excuse.

"I had to come here." He allows himself to sink deeper into the blank reflection staring back at him. "There was something I had to do."

He steps back now, trying to regain his balance and find a way onto the front foot—what was the last thing he said before she accused him of this, of engineering his own downfall? They have been in the last frantic stages of getting dressed for the party, the few guests who have managed to show up already milling about downstairs amidst the muffled noise of greeting one another and their own two children—teenagers—seating them at the dining room table, offering them cocktails or glasses of wine. The noise echoes terribly in this old stone house, so even five or six people talking at once could make it seem as if an actual party were underway. She had been about to go downstairs and attend to the guests, while he finished buttoning his shirt, and his own misgivings about his work had started them off—what was it he said?

*Maybe Rafa was right. Maybe it was a mistake. No one is coming to the unveiling—no one will see it.*

Yes, that was all it took, finally putting into words what had been troubling him the past three or four weeks, the sense that he has made the biggest wrong turn of his career, dragging them both here to this quaint and isolated village in the south of France to work on his new piece, an installation at the very peak of the huge outcropping of rock—not quite a mountain, though some of the locals do refer to it as such—on which the village is perched. Along with the painstaking attention to detail involved in executing the final finishing touches, along with the exuberance and satisfaction of completing the work, had come the slow realization that he has taken a very big risk in locating the piece at the top of a largely inaccessible chunk of granite, miles from the nearest town of any size. He has taken the view that if he built it, they would come, such has been the weight of his reputation in the world of modern conceptual art within the past fifteen years. But maybe Rafa was right. Raphaël de Guttierez, his manager back in New York, who had told him he was about to make the biggest mistake a modern artist could ever make. "Don't go off into the wilderness. You leave the scene, the patrons, you get out of touch. People forget." And now, tonight, the evening of the unveiling, he has been presented with tangible evidence that there is no *scene* here in Entrevoir. The guests who have arrived include primarily a few of their local friends they have met since moving to Entrevoir nine months ago, as well as a couple of the has been painters who come here to dabble in oils amongst the hills of the surrounding countryside—old codgers whose work is a living, breathing cliché from a century or two ago. Even Raphaël couldn't make it tonight. He is curating this week at a new multi-artist multimedia mash up in Brooklyn featuring several bleeding edge talents who are likely to get a nice mention in the Sunday *Times* cultural calendar and probably even an above the fold review. Rafa of course had duly mailed the hand-lettered parchment invitations to the unveiling here in Entrevoir to his list of wealthy and influential patrons in New York and London and around the world, and no less than a dozen of them RSVP'ed, but now it looks as if none of those who did will bother to show.

"We've tried things you wanted to do before," she is saying, sensing his imbalance, pressing her advantage, "and they haven't turned out very well."

He has to give her credit—they have been married seventeen years now, and she knows exactly which words will do the most damage, every time. She knows him as if

3

she *is* him. Marya, his lovely Marya, dark and lovely and still filled with all the danger that has lured him to her and kept him off balance over all these years. Which is what he must have wanted, what he must have known in his deepest inmost self when he met her: that she would always be a challenge to him, would always make him second-guess himself, feel that gnawing anxious empty pit in his stomach that makes him brood and pace and sit in coffee houses and stay up all night in his studio conjuring the breakthrough idea behind his next masterpiece of ideological, conceptual, phenomenological, highly experiential . . . art. Or what passes for art these days. Jacob grew up a painter, classically trained and naturally gifted. He could draw beautifully from the time he was three, completely breathtaking pencil still lifes he would draft on scraps of paper his mother gave him, portraits so stunning by the time he was six that even his father, an insurance salesman from a small Midwestern city, knew that he had no other choice but to nurture the boy's talent—teachers would call Jacob a prodigy—and so after Jacob graduated from high school his father allowed him to abstain from college and go directly to New York to live out his vision.

But Jacob doesn't paint much any more. And when he does, he no longer displays the work, or bothers to try and sell it. It would only cheapen the value of his "real" work—those absurd and yet sometimes absolutely gorgeous manifestations of high concept social commentary he has become the master of cranking out, one after another. Installations in the most unlikely places—ephemeral pieces such as his last exhibited work in a refrigerated meat-packing plant in Queens, which juxtaposed the bleeding sliced-open carcasses of sows and cattle with shimmering rays of sunlight he channeled through the killing machines and notches of the animals' spines. At the very end of the line the patrons had been confronted by a full-on view of an eviscerated cow belly, with most of the organs still in place, illuminated by stunning pallid sunlight directed in a spotlight effect through a precisely placed system of mirrors and lenses, as if the act of even viewing such an atrocity were being judged by the eyes of God. The installation had only been in place for a month, but the time constraint and the publicity from the strong warnings at the entrance to the exhibit space urging viewers to consider carefully whether they wanted to subject themselves to such a "deeply disturbing" experience, had served to build the fervor around the piece to a reservation-only waiting list of art world high rollers and cultural cognoscenti.

Jacob's work has always been about light. Even when he was still painting and first met Marya, his canvases were mainly an effort to bottle the most transitory effect a ray of light may have had on the stainless steel counter of a fast food restaurant, a derelict housing project, or a woman's shoe. He will never forget the first words Marya spoke to him, at one of his initial solo exhibits in a basement tavern on the surliest edge of the East Village: "You must see with great vision—I never met a painter who could see like that." With those words, and with those eyes of hers, she had him hooked.

But that is not what she is saying now. Now she says, "You know your works are installations. They have to be presented in the right place. Where people can *see* them."

"This is the right place. For this piece."

"Maybe. But there's nobody here. If you wanted to move to France, we could have at least lived in Paris, where there are still a few galleries and some semblance of an art scene—not to mention *people*." She turns her back and steps away from him now, about to let him fall. Getting the last word in before she heads downstairs to meet the guests. "Yes, maybe Paris, instead of this God-forsaken rock."

It is not God-forsaken—she is wrong here, for the first time maybe, she is absolutely wrong. This is why he has brought them here, to this obscure village he has chosen, to place himself at the top of this mountain, where he has attempted to construct a work of art that will enable human beings to see the face of God. Of course, he has never mentioned this to anyone, especially Marya, or Rafa. Unlike most other modern conceptual artists, he leaves the commentary to others, lets the curators and critics decide what his works are supposed to mean. It is the mystery of the piece that sells it, brings it to life. And this, in his view, is what has distinguished him from other less prominent artists of his day—he leaves the mystery in place, lets each viewer of the piece decide what it means to them. Most of his fellow artists weave long commentaries to be printed in pamphlets the viewers receive at the door of their exhibits, or on a placard next to the piece, explaining in droning, pretentious technical language the "metastory" behind the work, and in many cases this conceptual blather is more artfully conceived and compelling than the installation itself, for it is the *concept* that sells these days—the high-minded social commentary that makes or breaks the work.

This new piece, titled *Entrevoir,* which he has been constructing the past nine months, and dreaming about on and off for the past thirteen years, goes beyond anything he has ever attempted to create before. He has been thinking of it as his masterpiece, the defining work of his life. Something that will *not* be taken down after a month. Something that will live on the top of this mountain forever, that people will be journeying to see a hundred years from now. He *likes* that it is in a difficult place to reach—that is part of the allure. Maybe it will never receive the initial fanfare most of his other works receive, but over time—yes—after decades perhaps, it will be recognized as one of the greatest works of art ever created by man. To do something like that, he has had to take some chances, coming here to a tiny village in the south of France, hiking up a rock-strewn path to the wind-blown peak of the summit this village is perched upon day after day, purchasing the acreage from the ancient family of Provençal sheep-herders who have owned it since the sixteenth century. He has envisioned the viewers of this piece as pilgrims in a way, journeying here because they are paying homage to something bigger than themselves, coming away from the experience transformed forever. They have to be willing to work for the experience, knowing full well that they are in for an ordeal, willing to sacrifice a part of themselves for something everlasting in return. So, yes, it shouldn't really be a surprise to him that the usual cast of characters who flock to his installations in Manhattan, Brooklyn, London, Moscow, and Shanghai haven't bothered to turn up to the unveiling—perhaps they never will. So be it. If this is the worst mistake he has ever made, at least he will have failed in a grand manner. And he can always go back to what he did before, go back to Manhattan and regurgitate more of those extravagant deconstructive gestures that have earned him so much wealth and adulation.

Now he simply wants to bask in the feeling of accomplishment, fill his mind with the pure emotion of what this work really means to him, what he has felt each day as he trudged up the windswept path that leads to the top of that rock a hundred meters above their heads. The path that leads to that rocky plateau where he has situated the piece is treacherous in places, with views of the town and river below that make him feel as if he will be lifted off the rock and cast down, into the chasm of open space.

When he first began planning the piece, he wondered if he might have underestimated the engineering challenges of constructing it. The ground there on the plateau is not altogether level, and for weeks he had grave concerns that he had chosen the wrong spot. When he tried to place the foundations for the first of the pylons that serve to anchor the framework of the installation, he had to try at least a dozen different spots before he found enough solid footing to support the load. And then there is the wind. He had always expected the wind to be an integral part of the work—the interplay between the wind and the light. But he had not counted on such consistently high winds, always streaming across the exposed face of the rock, drawn there by the temperature gradient between the Mediterranean some thirty miles to the south and the first jagged peaks of the high Alps to the north. He had underestimated all of these things, had wrestled with the elements through winter and into the spring, had almost given up on several occasions when the framework and all it held had come crashing to the ground. And yet it is finished. It exists. It lifts him up, to the top of that mountain, up and out of himself. He stares at the back of Marya's head, as she turns to leave him, and he remembers again what he experienced earlier this afternoon when he reflected upon the completed piece for the final time before the unveiling, gazing at it in absolute peace. Once more he is lifted up, to the top of that mountain and beyond it, lifted away from himself he closes his eyes and feels his body falling away his body no longer his anymore he is rising up and out of it, he is lifted away to a place that may not exist for he sees now in his head and in his only certain knowing a field of stars laid out before him, a tapestry of gems each strung upon a latticework of light, spread out upon a faintly pulsating violet web these jewels are glowing, casting forth their lights of every color to him. As he scans this field of light, he is drawn to one of them, one of the jewels pulls him towards it. There is no fear, no dread or longing, for he no longer has a body, nothing he can fear to lose. In sense or sensitivity he has shaped his shifting nowhere self to some other realm inside him or inside of every other. Confined no more restricted dragged and pulled away inside a genuine unveiling thoughts assembled tossed aside the shell that once constrained him rent asunder the body he once called his own and named himself as this no longer serves him. Now a new thing—the full-force understanding that I am not the body, I am not the shell that served me. The veil of the temple is rent asunder, cast aside and opened to reveal. The jewel which pulls him towards it is but another form, another life he has chosen to conceal.

The gem he has lent his focused consciousness to slips around soft and unseemly shape shifting form from the inside out his own focused light of awareness shining through this jewel is enormous now that he has slipped himself inside through his own projecting infiltration of light. Though his own light of awareness is shining through this he can sense another light that builds itself out from the center of this being he has now become. His form in this life he has slipped into is immense—he does not know how he can be aware of this, how he can relate its size to anything outside himself, but somehow he can *feel* it, and in his own subjective awareness it extends to what he might consider to be like unto the diameter of the entire Earth itself, this star he is some nine thousand miles across, twenty-seven thousand miles around, and yet… he is all of it, and it is not a planet, not the Earth, but a distant star he has become. The veil of the temple is rent asunder. He is not the body, no longer the body he has known, the one who painted the paintings, who loved that woman who turned her back to him, who draped upon that mountaintop a curtain of glittering wind-blown evanescent fabric designed to transform sunlight and moonlight into a shimmering display of pure extenuating color and delight. He is no longer that one, now he is this—a burning threshold tumult of nuclear particles ripped into ions stripped of their atomic bonds, an incredibly dense white hot plasma of carbon and oxygen generating heat and light not through nuclear fusion as most normal stars do, now only through the density of its electrons pressing so tightly together they can barely move. He knows from his awareness that it was not always thus. Millions of years ago he had been a star of normal type, the size of Earth's sun, which had cycled through millions of years of brightly shining fusion, pressing out light and heat from his essential self until he finally grew and grew to become a red giant larger than the orbit of Jupiter at one point and then shedding his layers of excess lifting shining mass and leaving behind only this carbon oxygen plasma core pressed down and left to cool himself for untold billions upon billions of years—he has been shining here now forever he has sent his light out upon the partner star his mate now blue hot and locked together in orbit with him as well as another much smaller red dwarf star their son who orbits them both together far away, they have danced this dance together now for millions upon millions of years and will go on dancing together here forevermore. He had once been the brightest of the three, the family here together, Sirius B they call him on Earth, now his former mate Sirius A shines brightest in the night, but in his own time, when he was largest when he ruled the skies, he was far brighter than the one they call A now, and the one they know nothing of, their son, has always been too dim to be detected on that planet far away. There are rocky planets here too with them, some dragged and diverted in their orbits between the constantly swinging duet of himself and his brightly shining mate, others orbiting far away from both, beyond even the orbit of the red dwarf third star of the system. In the days of the ages ago one of those planets in the furthest reaches beyond the red dwarf son held a race of enlightened beings who was forced to flee to Earth when he expanded 120 million years ago to his greatest extent as a giant menacing crimson star and scorched their world, they sometimes do return here for it is their spiritual home though they have lived on Earth since then. He was their father, the brighter of the two that gave them light, and it is really him they worshipped when they bowed down to Isis, the wife, now A, and Osiris, the husband, now B, and Horus, the tiny Son/Sun those on Earth have never seen, their hieroglyph showing star and planet and triangle of the holy triad he once reigned upon here. In his density he reigns here still for his tightly wound up mass is yet the focus for all the bodies swinging around him in orbit, residual motions still prevailing from the time so long ago when he was the father, Osiris, the largest and brightest of the three. The massiveness and density of this body is oppressive to him and enlightening all the same. He feels himself radiating, clutched together all the sacred members of his body so tightly wound that they cannot help but send out an intensity of light his former self could never hope to know. Tightly packed the ions and white particulate matter shines and writhes in blocks stacked and shining one into another stacked and packed and pressed together all as one. His awareness of his conscious self is so invisibly focused here in this body radiating light... how could he be here in this densely packed white bright sphere of burning plasma light and on that mountain top and in that stone-floored room seeing the back of Marya's head turning away from him all the same?

This thought which has reached him in this jewel of light lifts him up again and out from that far away star—up and above the tapestry woven of a web of brightly colored gems, each of them stars in and of themselves, and maybe something more than that, perhaps each of them is another part of himself, another focused aspect of his consciousness, another life he has lived or is yet to live.

He falls into another one; from the grid of woven violet luminosity he falls headlong into a glittering godsent gemstone onto another mountain top again he slips into another self another sliding shimmer sheath of form; his awareness tightens itself within and sends its beacon forthwith through this other self into the world which surrounds it and sees through the eyes of another being whom he was again once more: a boy on a dark dirt road being led to the top of a mountain. Around him are several older men in sackcloth and vestments all in white, their waists tied round about with sashes laced with gold. Several men, priests all of them, *magi*—the word comes to him now—all of them leading him to the top of the mountain along with acolytes in a procession where he will be allowed to enter the cult to which they all belong, will be deigned to enter in to the mysteries which they all must pass through to gain entrance to the privileged vision which they all must share with one another. There are two animals here with them, trudging along at his side, a bull and a ram, braying, the bull led by one of the priests holding a rope that passes through a ring slung through its nose. Smell of animals defecating in their fear and the priest—the *lan-lirira*—who crushes the plants in the mortar and pestle even as they go, as they proceed to the sacred top of the mountain where the *lan* ceremony will take place, the magus to his right is crushing the floral material with mortar and pestle, crushing the petals of jasmine lavender and sage into the holy milk of *haoma*—the words are all here, all these strange words of the ritual are with him as if he never left this other mountain top in Pasargadae where his initiation into the sacred mystery once upon a time ago is taking place.

They have led him from the *pairidaeza,* the walled garden paradise in the royal palace on the valley floor below, up the rocky trail in the cold open air to the *ayadana*—the *kušukum,* the *hapidamuš*—the mountain temple where this ritual will envelope him. More than anything, he feels cold. Not fear—he is numb to the fear, he has been anticipating this moment for more than a year now, since they first accepted him as an acolyte into the mysteries, since they brought him away from his family of sheep herders in the arid high plateau of Dasht-I Kavir. The cold of the night mountain air under this deep black blanket of stars and the crescent moon—everyone knows, even those laymen who will never be blessed with the opportunity to undergo the mystery rites, that the initiation can only be performed beneath a crescent moon. There is nothing else between him and the cold night air but the drapery of the simple scratchy sackcloth which clothes him. The wind works its way in between the gaping holes at the armpits and up around his naked knees and legs. Amidst the cold and the florid scent of *haoma,* which he assumes he will have to drink, he catches a glimpse of one of the other acolytes—one he has seen in the palace temple before. A girl, his age or younger. There are very few girls or women around the parts of the palace where they allow him to go, but he has seen her, glancing at him the same way she is now, her dark eyes drawn up in shame, catching him once with their obsidian darkness, then quickly stealing away.

The procession comes to a halt. Looking, in the valley below, he can see the palace and the city that surrounds it—smaller than Persepolis forty miles to the south, the new capital, which Xerxes commissioned in his arrogance and grandeur—yet still an impressive sight, its silver walls lit by torches, its temple gates towering over the mud huts of the villagers squatting at its heel. His favorite part of living at the palace temple since coming here from his own village has been the trumpet calls that serve to announce the hours of ceremony through each day. He will be napping on his straw mat or fetching water for the noontime meal and suddenly the trumpets will blare a staccato clarion call, each hour a different piercing melody and rhythm, maybe forty trumpeters or more, announcing the movement of the king from one chamber to the next, or the arrival of some general or ambassador from a mission in the far west. Here now there is only silence, at the top of the mount, only the sound of his own shallow breathing can he hear.

He stands in the middle of a circle of priests, stepping around him in a slow and retrograde procession, and the girl now steps forth—the acolyte who will disrobe him. One of the priests stands before him and intones:

"Son of man, come forth with me now and undertake the Divine mystery of initiation into new life which begins again without sin."

These are the words, he knows, which begin the ceremony he has been instructed in, over the weeks of fasting and preparation, words he has memorized as a response to every step of the ancient rite. He feels the words come out of his mouth without even thinking of them—they are an automatic response:

"Abide with me in my soul; leave me not, that I may be initiated and that the HOLY SPIRIT may breathe within me."

He has been trained in this and tutored, in this moment he must demonstrate his purity, for as he raises his arms to the stars and utmost heavens above him, the crescent moon flickering its silvery pale impression of the highest light upon him, the girl moves close by his side, her breath in his ear and the dark emptying pools of her eyes draining him of all emotion, he must maintain his chastity, the lower parts of himself must not react, as her body brushes itself against him as she lifts his robe up and over his shoulders, off of him, exposing his naked flesh to the sobering midnight wind on the top of the mountain. He mustn't make a sound now or a move. Standing perfectly still he must breathe, inhale and exhale in a slow and steady manner as she anoints him with the milk of *haoma*, oily and thick as cream in the first pale light of the morning, her hands spreading it over his shoulders and torso, down to his buttocks and the front of him below. He must not make a move.

Closing his eyes, he feels her hands upon him, spreading the milky oil over every contour of his body; he focuses on his breathing, as they have instructed, on the Spirit which is filling him, on the inside, focusing on what is within rather than what is without will enable him to endure this and accept the blessing of a new birth in the mysteries of the Spirit of the Lord. Eyes closed, he can hear the slow shuffling footsteps of the *magi* as they circle round about him, he can hear the heavy breathing of the bull.

"Cast off the garments and anoint this son of man, O priestess, and on this throne, prepare him to enter the chamber."

Eyes open, body wet with oil, he looks into her eyes—the one he sees, he has seen a thousand times before. Her eyes widen and meet his for a moment, then she turns to join the other *magi* in the dance of the procession.

He takes his seat on the marble throne, naked, the stone cold and wet against his thighs and back and buttocks, the night wind swirling across the top of the mount above him. He closes his eyes again for a moment, to gather himself. Now it truly begins. He has been instructed in the ceremony, up to this point. What comes beyond this has been purposefully left to his own imagination. He has heard stories, rumors of what trials will come next, and he has already endured three rites for the neophyte grades leading up to this most important ritual—levels of Catechesis he has already achieved, these being *Raven, Secret One,* and *Warrior.*

She returns now with the mortar—perhaps they have added something to the *haoma,* while he was not looking?

The priest, the leader of the rite, whose name is Gaumata, pronounces these words:

"Drink now, son of man, partake of the sacred *haoma,* with which your body has been anointed. As within, so without."

He takes the mortar from her, a carved stone bowl that fits within his palm, and lifts it to his mouth. He knows he mustn't change his expression, no matter how vile this broth he drinks will taste to him. He must not react in a negative manner to anything that happens as the initiation unfolds, and he must be prepared to endure anything.

He has been able to smell it a bit as she spread it on his body, and now he puts the bowl to his lips and lets it slip into him, the liquid cool, flecked with leaves and sweet tasting shriveled things that must be flower petals—there is a milky mixture of bitter and sickly sweet that makes him want to gag and cough the first gulp up again—but he mustn't. To control the gag reflex he looks into her eyes and thinks of this as a connection directly with her. That's it. He is taking her into him, he is becoming one with her. And more than that, he knows, this ceremony is supposed to bring him to the point where he may become one with God.

With that thought in mind, he takes another sickly sweet gulp, drinks it all down, crushed leaves, petals and silky white fluid.

She steps away from him, and bids him to rise now from the throne, leads him past the circle of priests who stop their dance and follow them along with Gaumata towards a long trench that has been hollowed out over time, in the rutted earth.

Naked, shivering wet and cold, vaguely nauseated from partaking of the *haoma*, he stands before them. The *magi* have continued their low chanting, words he cannot understand, a droning backdrop to the words Gaumata now pronounces.

"We are each HIS offspring—do you suppose that our Father would suffer His own son to be *enslaved*?"

His mind whirls, he is seeing strange colors, perhaps a mild hallucinogenic effect of the *haoma*. He was not instructed what to do or say at this point, so, he wisely holds his tongue, says nothing, stands perfectly still in the freezing wind.

More from Gaumata: "You are bearing a God with you, though you know it not. Come my son, duly prepared and purified for initiation into this sacred rite, come now and enter the chamber, the Holy of Holies, for THE VEIL OF THE TEMPLE IS RENT ASUNDER. Know then, that thou art not the body, thou art God."

Gaumata points to the trench, and he knows that he must step towards it, perhaps they will throw him in it, and then do what?

"My son, this night at midnight thou shalt be purified and born again for eternity. Hear therefore, and believe what is true. Pray with me and say these words I say."

He knows this is his cue—in every other rite he has passed through in the three prior stages, this has been his cue to repeat what the high priest is saying, and as Gaumata pronounces these words, he says them as if they are together pronouncing them with one mouth, at one and the same time:

"Abide with me in my soul; leave me not, that I may be initiated and that the Holy Spirit may breathe within me."

His voice has become hoarse in the night wind as he says this holy prayer, following along with the priest.

"I a man born of mortal womb, am this day begotten again by Thee, out of so many myriads rendered immortal in this hour by the will of God in His abounding goodness."

Gaumata gestures again, and he sees that he must step down into the trench. He lowers himself into the hole and lies down on the wet earth, staring up at Gaumata and the other priests encircling the violet sky above him.

"Pray with me and say these words I say: I approach the confines of Death and lie down in the threshold of the chamber. I am carried through all the elements and I will return again. In the middle of the night I will see the Sun, gleaming in radiant splendour. I approach into the presence of the gods below and the gods celestial and worship before their faces."

The priests lower a board over the trench, now casting him into deeper darkness. There are only a few gaps in the board where the pale light of the crescent moon can make its way through. He can hear them treading on the dirt above him, smell the sickening scent of *haoma* and feel the wet earth on his naked back and legs—he has clasped his hands together over his chest to keep his arms out of the muck.

21

With the board in place, he no longer repeats Gaumata's words, but listens instead as the hooves of the bull clatter onto the heavy wooden planks above his face.

Gaumata's voice again speaks. "Behold, I have told you things which, although you have heard them, you must not understand."

The bull gives forth a terrible low groaning sound, resonating through its chest and lungs, as its flesh is torn apart. He cannot see this, only hears the rending tearing sound as of a curtain torn and ripped from its pinions. The priests call out to each other as they set upon the huge beast, slicing it open with their knives. And now the blood of the beast that has been ripped open starts trickling down and dripping on him, through the cracks in the plank above him—hot warm heavy liquid pouring through now into this tomb he is trapped in. He closes his eyes to shield them, and can only feel the hot blood pouring down upon his naked skin, warming him, covering him in a bath of blood. He is soaking in it, the blood pouring over him, drenching him in its hot metallic scent, and with his eyes closed he feels himself lifted out of his shaking body, colors of magenta and gold spiraling across his field of sight within, enveloped in a heated womb of blood and warmth now, descending within himself and lifted up through the colors, through the dawning of an orgiastic light within. The blood is seeping into his mouth and nose as he struggles still to breathe, seeps into his mouth and he drinks it, must swallow some to keep himself from choking, there is so much blood.

This is what it must feel like to be dying, drenched in blood and choking, eyes closed and seeing only spiral effigies of light. This is what it must feel like to step out of your body and die.

Once again he is lifted up, his secret self that watches himself is lifted back and away from the being whose body is being drenched and bathed with blood, communicant with the Holy Spirit, he lifts his awareness away out of recognition remembrance and fear it is lifted from the boy and sails outward back and away from this mountain top tomb out into the paralyzing black expanse of space again to drift upon the endlessness, the effortlessness of his own awareness loosed upon the wide open ocean of mind without matter. Yet it only lasts an instant; in the next extent of a ticking timepiece he is in another place, another moment presents himself to his present self to conjure a life again anew.

He finds himself standing in a field of tall grass, a wire fence and a cornfield off to the left. But it is not himself any longer—he looks down at his legs and sees that the legs are those of a teenaged girl in a skirt, with white bobby socks and black patent leather shoes. The skirt is a pale blue and the girl's legs are pink in the late afternoon sun. Her hair is blond and it blows across her shoulder in the light wind that chases across the rolling green landscape of the open field. The tall prairie grass and the corn rustle with the breeze. He is both watching this girl and one with the girl at the same time. She feels a surge of excitement as she looks up into the blue gulf of sky above her—a plane is approaching, a light prop plane easing down out of the clouds. This is exhilarating—it's her father's plane she is watching, and it thrills her to see it approaching the field to land. Her father is a pilot, he flies this plane for a living, carrying cargo and sometimes passengers across the open fields from the small town where they live to cities far away. He has the feeling, watching this, being this girl, that this is happening in the 1950s, perhaps the late fifties. There is no way to be sure and no way to understand how he could know this, it is all just a feeling he has as he is watching the scene even as he is in it.

The girl begins to run towards the place where the plane is coming in to land. Her father is flying the plane, and he is coming home—as she is running though, she senses something is wrong. The plane is too low, the angle it is coming in at is off somehow, too steep. She stops running, stands still in the breeze and watches, as everything decelerates into a slow-motion nightmare inevitable and wrenching the breath out of her as she watches. The sound of the engine shifts from a droning buzz to a low whirling sound, down a full octave from where her ear knows it should be—and with this dip in the pitch of the engine noise she sees the nose of the plane tilt downward... the plane is going down, straight down. She runs towards it again and as she runs she sees the nose of the plane heading straight for the earth, in stop action it seems, barreling down upon the grassy field at an angle all wrong, running towards it she hears the engine rev one last time and falter, sees the plane disappear into a crumpled heap upon the field and feels the impact of the machine and her father with it as it buries itself into the ground.

She keeps on running, keeps running towards him, and he feels himself watching this running with her, running towards something he doesn't want to see or understand. His awareness, the consciousness of the watcher, who is watching the scene in the field and is within the girl living it at the same time, pulls itself *back,* away from the scene, away from the girl, and at the same time keeps running, with eyes closed, the awareness which he is—the watcher—keeps running, and when he opens his eyes again he sees that he is running down a long corridor, a passageway—a gallery with marble floors and statues lined up on either side as he passes by them. But these are not statues, he sees, as he slows himself to a stop, they are something more. They are images frozen in time, people slowed down to a stationary moment, still-life impressions of various people each of them inhabiting a scene that has been slowed down to a fixed motion picture frame of a life.

There are so many of them—the gallery stretches before him as far as his eye can see. He turns to look behind him and the corridor is endless that way too. He could run and run forever and not reach the end of it. He steps towards one of them, brings it into clearer focus. It is a frozen statue scene of where he has just been—the plane, still hanging there in the air in the moment before impact, with the girl watching in that tranquil yet horrible field. As he keeps his focus on it something very strange begins to happen. The airplane begins to move, ever so slightly, and the girl in the pale blue dress begins to run towards it. And as he keeps his awareness on it a moment longer, he feels himself begin to be pulled within it, start to come together with this scene and draw into the body of that little girl.

He shakes himself away, forcibly jerks his awareness back from the scene. He does not want to go back there and re-live it. He pulls himself away and begins to run again. Running down the passageway, the gallery, but running to where?

There is nowhere else to go. The gallery goes on forever. After a moment more of running he begins to slow down, turns around again and sees it going on forever the other way. Deciding now that the only way out is through one of these still-life holograms of a life, he looks at the many visions surrounding him in this part of the corridor—all black and darkness of empty space beyond the images on either side. There is one he feels drawn to, an image of a young man staring out the window of a house at the sea: He moves towards it, and the tiny waves along the shore begin to tug away. He continues forward and feels himself being drawn within the young man's body, a younger man than he, feels himself full of energy, full of life, within this body and pulling his awareness within now sees through the very selfsame eyes of this young man, standing at the broad windowpane of the house, gazing out at the vast expanse of the sea. Not a sea, though, an ocean. He cannot be sure how he knows this, but it is definitely an ocean, can smell the salt air and can sense that the nearest land on the other end of this water is thousands of miles away.

The water is glowing. He sees that now, it is shimmering with an unearthly blue that radiates a crowning tinge of gold which casts a spell upon him as if his spine were being played by fingertips drawn along the strings of a harp. The water runs up along the shore and crashes against a tall formation of black rock at the far end of the beach. There is no one else around, as far as he can see in either direction. The sky is a strange almond color he has never seen in skies on Earth, and yet he feels as if he is home, the only home he has ever known.

This body feels comfortable to him, a taut young man's body, full of life. He turns to look at the house—his house. Its furnishings are spare but entirely comfortable and familiar to him, not unlike those he would expect in a beach house on Earth. There is a low, long table in front of a couch where he spends time relaxing, framed artwork on the walls, and beyond this large room with its high ceilings is a kitchen, open to the room and its view of the water. He goes towards the table and reaches for a book there—perhaps that will tell him more about where he is? He can see that even the table and the book—all the objects in the room—emit an unearthly glow. Shimmering, as if they are formed of a less dense species of matter. He tries to pick the book up, but his hand passes *through* it. Is it real? Is this place real, or something he is dreaming? He tries to pass his hand through the low table, to experience the odd sensation of the electric charge he just felt when his hand passed through the wavering energy of an object. This time he is less successful, his hand bumps against the table—maybe because he is thinking about it more. He senses another presence in the room with him; watching him.

He turns about and sees the outline of a human form across the room, a glowing shadow-form, not quite there. He takes a step towards it and it comes together more completely, shimmers and shines with the light of dozens of tiny blue stars lit up within it. Perhaps this being has brought him here?

"Where am I?" he asks it, the first thing that comes to mind.

No words come forth in reply, but there is an answer, already in his head: "Everywhere."

"What is this place then? Why am I seeing it now?"

"Always questions…" The being seems amused somehow. "Your consciousness, your spirit creates it— your higher self."

"That doesn't tell me where this is, or who you are."

The being seems to change shape now, dissolving its human form into more of a loose sphere, hundreds of blue stars shining at the fringes of it.

"You are being raised up. Your awareness is expanding."

And then, as if to show him what this means, the being grows larger, suddenly grows to fill the room. In doing so, it passes through him in somewhat the same way he felt his hand pass through that book... a gentle merging, a crisp electric current intersecting his flesh. His eyes close and he can feel the blue stars all about him, the shimmering golden light of this other being flooding through him. The being isn't speaking to him, but something is being communicated to him nevertheless. He can feel various tones, various colors being transmitted through the cells of his body, directly downloading some kind of information. He can hear the colors coming through him, blue and violet rivers of sound silver gold raiment of electric bells and organ pipe vibrations cyan deep emerald and gold. He can see the sounds flowing through him changing tones along a scale ascending up and up throughout the ladders and stairways of his mind merging along the path arising to this being he has been brought together with, sounds and colors coming through as some kind of words, each sound is the same as a color and the same as a texture and the same as a word. In ancient days these beings may have given these things names, when they had to stoop to call these things to one another with spoken words, before they grew to simply grow together this way now. These are words he cannot understand and yet he knows they bring him meanings, carry new awareness to him. He can barely make them out as they pass right through him *Ong emon atosh em evobah olotro phremo ulatah vremo ba nataqa* what does this mean?

The words and sounds and colors are the same, each a different variation of a frequency, thousands of gradations across a spectrum energy of light *atawa gref movakcas lant anat antat qwotos cav prefat mab olate oul gre bxi paaq jemal emon atosh em evobah olotro Ong* the words carry him forth ascending and expanding, raised up and exalted.

Something is coming through, some meaning he can coalesce in his head now, words he can understand:

"You chose to come back."

Chose to come back—here? To this beach house on a planet or a time so far away from his own life he had been living? And this thought produces something that feels like a weight tugging at his feet and the center of his chest, pulling him down. He feels inside him a physical heaviness, a solid weight, as if his arms and legs are going dead, some heavy stone that is dragging him *down,* a heavy tugging tingling feeling like an arm that has fallen asleep after having lain on it too long, but the tingling is spreading throughout his body, the heaviness pulling him down and making his eyes go blank. And then he is back—back standing in his own body, or what has been his own, the body of Jacob, standing again in the stone upper bedroom of the house in Entrevoir, watching as Marya turns away from him, staring at the placid and lovely skin at the base of her neck, her hair pulled up in a chignon style for the party, as she is taking the step still she was about to take when he first felt himself launched upward into whatever it was that has just happened to him.

He can hear again the sounds of the small party downstairs—the guests having just arrived, five or six of them at most it seems—someone laughing at a joke someone has made, his son's voice rising to greet the punch line, his son always courteous, gracious even at this young age, a teenager comfortable in social settings with adults, accustomed to the dinner parties and cocktail hours his parents have always dragged him to. His daughter pouring glasses of wine; he can hear the glasses clink. And Marya turning her back on him, leaving him. As she has done before.

He sees a strand of loose hair at the base of her neck, which has already fallen from the chignon, and he can sense what she is thinking, or maybe he simply attributes this to her, projects it onto her: His new piece—she hates it. She hates being here, hates having to have moved away from Manhattan, hates whatever his new work is; though he has not even showed it to anyone yet, he has given her clues as to what it is like. She must be secretly glad in a way that the unveiling party is failing, that his new work is already a flop before it's even been shown to a single soul. Because if this little excursion here he has dragged them on, wasting a year of their lives, is a failure, then he will be forced to see that they never should have left New York and they can go back to where they belong and get on with their lives once again.

He knows she is thinking these things, as she turns to take the first step down the stairs, because they have had arguments about this before. Discussions, she would call

31

them—but to him, they have felt more like arguments, accusations. Maybe that's what drove him out of his mind just now, into that crazy dim hallucination, out of his body, whatever it was—did he black out for a moment? Maybe he has not been getting enough sleep, racing to finish everything on the installation in time for the unveiling.

It could have been some kind of strange *déjà vu*. That's more what it felt like, not an hallucination. All of it felt entirely real—like he had been to all of those places before. That odd feeling of having done this before, having been in this new place already, getting a strange glimpse of knowing exactly what will happen next, what the other person is about to say.

And it all happened in an instant—all at once really. Perhaps it had been just a momentary thought, a kind of daydream taking him away from the strain of their argument, the disappointment of the unveiling and the fact that he has just realized that Marya hates his new work.

Yes, many thoughts can be folded into a single instant. In this very moment watching Marya take her next step, before her next footfall on the burnished stone floor, he is already thinking again about his work, that magnificent work of art he has been imagining for years and constructing for months high on the mountain top hundreds of feet above their heads. To get there, you must climb a rocky path, very steep but not rugged, a climb that will leave you winded by the time you get to the top, but he has always conceived of it as a pilgrim's journey, an arduous adventure to see this work. The journey there, the physical exertion, is part of the experience of it. And so, there at the plateau at the top of the rock upon which the village of Entrevoir resides, he has laid out a labyrinth for the visitor to his work to undertake. He envisions it now in his mind's eye, as he has imagined it while he created it, and as he saw it when he finished it and walked the completed path himself earlier today.

When the visitor arrives at the plateau, she sees the installation spread out before her—why she? Has he been imagining Marya viewing it, what her reaction will be?

It no longer matters. He knows now that she already hates it.

When the visitor arrives, she—maybe it is some other woman now—is drawn in to the work by the path moving forward around the outside of the plateau, encircling one edge of the perimeter, with stunning views of the town and the valley and the river winding far below. Then, at the far side of the plateau, the path turns back towards the entrance, back across the plateau, a stone path winding, twisting, turning back upon itself, enfolding the pilgrim into his work, bringing her within the experience, drawing her in to a certain mindset, a framework for understanding. He has designed the path so that each turning point within the labyrinth provides the visitor with an opportunity to contemplate the piece from a different angle, to experience a new and ever-changing play of light and wind on the ethereal curtains of metallic fabric on display. And each of these turning points are aligned with key astronomical events on various dates—the rising of the sun at the summer solstice, the setting of the sun on the winter solstice, the rising of Sirius at the spring equinox. Venus setting on the first day of fall.

Thinking about these celestial objects brings him back to an awareness of the heaviness he is feeling now with his feet firmly planted on the stone floor of this room. The dense torpor of having his awareness rooted in a body, weighed down by the solid curtain of his own flesh. He had been so light only an instant ago, in the beach house barely there, his body mostly a gleaming outline of form, a translucent container for his awareness. And in that corridor, that gallery of frozen holographs of lives he might have lived, he had been nothing more than awareness, nothing more than the watcher, a viewer with the potential of experiencing whatever it was he put his attention to. The bodies he moved in and out of were never him, the boy on the mountain top with those priests and the girl acolyte and that ill-fated bull. The girl running across the field to where her father's plane had just crashed. Even that star—the absolute density of burning hot plasma pressed in upon itself to the most tightly packed form imaginable—even that had been his body but never strictly him. He had been more like nothingness, more like a melody drifting on the wind… vibrations lifting him up again, pulling him with a ringing rushing sound up and out, away from the stone room and into that blank nothingness pedestal of glimmering light. The fear which held him back is no longer there anymore—he lets himself go where his soul will take him, lets himself slide into whatever density the watcher will lend to him on the next available shore.

Horns sounding—trumpets again, but this time a cruder version, sounded together and out of key, a melody without harmony, blaring amidst chanting cries of a multitude of people surrounding him in a vast plaza—no, not him, he realizes once again as he slips into awareness of this new body that she is a young woman, barely dressed, her hips and thighs covered in a rough and brightly colored cloth, her breasts nearly exposed by the sash that drapes a single shoulder and circles round her chest. Soles of her bare feet on the clay dirt of this immense public plaza. Thousands of people here surrounding her, calling out, chanting in rhythm words he has never heard before, but as familiar as an old nursery rhyme she remembers and can follow word for word:

Tiazque yehua xon ahuiacan. Annochipa tlalticpac. Zan achica ye nican! Tel ca chalchilnuitl no xamani, no teocuitlatl in tlapani, oo quetzalli poztequi. Annochipa tlalticpac zan achica ye nican. Ohuaya ohuaya! In her head she knows what this means—We will pass away. Not forever on Earth, only a brief time here! Even jades fracture; even gold ruptures, even quetzal plumes tear. Not forever on Earth, only a brief time here! Ohuaya ohuaya, they all chant together, trumpets blare, shells are cracked and sounds of wailing fill the air.

She looks up to the very top of the great stepped pyramid in front of her and sees high above the priests of the ceremony holding the warrior's heart aloft, lifting up the sanctified substance, flesh of the gods, the precious eagle-cactus fruit, dripping, blood pouring down upon the stones. Now the cries lift up, the people around her know the city will be saved another season, another battle has been won, another harvest will be reaped. The feeling wells up from these multitudes, surges up and lifts them all together, which is pride mingled with dread mingled with fear. The precious eagle-cactus fruit has been lifted out of the body of the warrior, the body of the god, which is one with it and one with us all. The precious body of the warrior has never died in vain, every warrior willingly goes, every sacrifice is in honor and remembrance, never pain. Priests high and mighty dressed in flailed skin dressed in blood never kill in vain. Every sacrifice is holy, every warrior never thought he would be slain. Every Awesome and Terrible Lord Who Fills One Up with Dread cut the hair of the warrior who became in remembrance an eagle-man raised upward to the Sun. In remembrance of the Sun the eagle-man gives his precious eagle-cactus fruit unto the Awesome and Terrible Lord.

We will pass away—not forever on this Earth, only a brief time here.

Even gold ruptures—even quetzal plumes tear.

They tear the eagle man limb from limb, they toss his horn beak down the steps a thousand feet tumbling down below and even so the trumpets blare drums beating, as they tear him limb from limb. Shells crack bones crack, bones break and crack upon the stone. Drums beat and chanting priests who wear the hair and skin of gods and eagles rising as they soar.

Ohuaya, ohuaya! In honor and remembrance of me.

And when his toppled body tumbled to the floor, the singing stops for a moment. Everything stops.

The priests bow down to the prince—to the Awesome and Terrible Lord. Whom she knows. She has known him, bodily has she known him, when he came to her village, across the waters, across the shore. She knows him and has been one with him—He came to her in her willingness to receive him, even as she was working on her craft, carving shells and arrow stones. He knows her and she has known him. And they all look to him now, the multitudes, looking as one, for what sign he shall give.

What sign shall he give?

He points. His finger pointing in her direction. Is he pointing at her? And then a name is called and in an instant soldiers move to put their hands on her. Her name has been called—Xilonen—a holy name, he has called her.

Why would he call her? She has already given her body to him, already opened herself unto her Lord, as he demanded. But that is not enough for him, or perhaps too much. Could it be that he is afraid of her, the knowledge of what he has done to her could be trouble even for him, for she has known in her heart of hearts that their union was not called for, not arranged in the way as it should have been, through the name of the mistress of the court.

It was done in a moment of silence—not called for—neither named nor announced nor acknowledged nor anointed. She has held it in her heart and so has he. Hoping it would come to nothing more. And here it has yes come to something more—here he has called her and betrayed her. To save himself from knowing and from being known.

The priestly brothers come for her, lay hands on her and bring her forth to the very steps of the temple strewn with blood and bones. Seven men have died today, seven warriors turned to gods. It is an honor to be called—she knows. It is an honor to be raised up with eagle wings unto the Lord. For those who rise up and give themselves up become one with the gods and become god. It is an honor, she knows, but still she cannot stifle the dread, the absolute terror of what is yet to come. This is why they call him, now shout his name as trumpets stir their clarion call: Awesome and Terrible Lord Who Fills One Up with Dread. The drums beat steady steady low and low the hordes of people cry out and the priest who takes her by the arm repeats her name for all to hear—Xilonen.

"Xilonen has been called unto the Lord," he says, raising her arm on high. "Ochpanitzli calls her heart and turns it into corn."

She looks, scans the faces in the crowd. Somewhere there her father, her mother must be watching her. Two younger brothers—what must they be thinking, knowing what is to come?

Drums beat louder now—trumpets call her home. People chant their dreadful song, loud and low: "We will pass away. Not forever on Earth, only a brief time here! Ohuaya, ohuaya!"

At the foot of the temple lie the flailed and broken bodies of the warrior gods, their bodies rent asunder, tossed down to the floor. The stones of the very first steps she walks up are slippery with their blood. The priests hold her arms, force her to take these steps. She always wondered what it would feel like to climb them and now she knows—no one would willingly go. No one could face this without fear. Even though she will soon become a goddess… the smell of blood is enough to make her retch.

She takes another step, then falls to her knees, wet with blood. They yank her up. Pull her arms from their sockets five hundred steps left to go, the city and the noise of the people fading down below. She goes with them, all the way to the top, head lolling to one side, eyes flutter closed. It would be better to pull herself from their grasp and die by falling, she could throw herself down the rocky steps. Better than what they have in store. She wrests her arm away but has no strength, can barely move it. They lift her up once more. Her legs move, how she does not know. They are all watching her, becoming a goddess now—her parents, will they be proud? Not so common for a lowly crafts maker, arrow head carver to be chosen; why, they will never know. In the village across the water, they will be the talk for years to come—mother of Xilonen, brother of Xilonen, father of Xilonen, who rose to become a god.

In this way at least, she will have become immortal, if not by the gods above or the gods below. She has never been sure about this—whether those warriors and maidens who give their lives become what they say they do. Now here she is at the top of the temple serpent mountain with the valley laid out before her, people small and trembling down below. Chanting reaching them on a wave of longing, tempered by the wind. She had never thought the wind could be so strong here.

At the temple stone, the altar, she is greeted by the Awesome and Terrible Lord. His body glistens, even these arms she has held, bare chest she has known. He nods at her, stares into her eyes—she has seen these eyes before. Obsidian eyes like Tezcatlipoca, like a smoking mirror. She bites her lip, utters his name—if she said something more, would it save her?

The other priests are here, four of them, their bodies adorned with the paper body streamers, flailed skins of the others who were here before. They will not let this stop. They lead her to the altar, lay her down upon the stone drenched in blood. She lays her head back, closes her eyes and gags—the smell of blood and consecrated flesh is too strong to bear. The wind howls in her ears. It may be the last thing she ever hears.

They begin the process of making her a god. The knives are sharp—when first they touch her, she hardly knows. She feels the skin from her calf and from her thigh fileted and stripped away. Eyes closed, she lets out a scream—they never hear it down below. The wind and drums and trumpets and screaming they all do there is loud enough, now she knows. They begin to pull her limb from limb. They continue flailing her tearing off her skin. She keeps her eyes closed—it is the only sense she can still control. All the others overwhelm her as the priests all set upon her, swiftly working, doing what they must do.

"Ohuaya, ohuaya," they chant. In honor and remembrance of me. She is being torn apart, flailed and skinned and torn limb from limb. She opens her eyes one last time and sees the dreadful sky above her, body flailing warm hot feeling of searing pain, the hands and knives upon her, holding her down, the terrible wind. Her body rent asunder—she sees him coming at her with a knife so big. Closes her eyes and feels it tear through the center of her chest, cracking her breasts apart. Drops her head to the side and feels them tugging at her heart. Still beating, she can hear the blood rush in her ear, but then the knives and hands are upon her and she is lighter now, rushing up now through the wind. She is gone—he, the watcher is gone now, carried away from this place by the grace of the light and the wind.

The wind and light shall carry him in remembrance of what he truly is. Not the body, not the mind. Not the sensations of that place. Only the feeling of undefined awareness being carried along by the wind. Only the awareness of being. There is blackness and no light. There is a rushing through a curtain that brushes against his side, gentle as an infant's touch. Someone calls his name. And a blurring, buzzing trembling feeling shudders through his legs and through his arms. The light grows brighter and surrounds him and he opens his eyes and hears his name called once again.

"Jiva. Why are you dawdling. Come with me!"

He feels his hand being grasped and looks around, in full sunlight now. The woman who said this and took his hand is much taller than he. He looks up to her and sees also that she is much older, he is only a child. And she is someone he knows, of course, someone he loves dearly. He knows her name and says it.

"Lakshmi, where are we going?"

"Aren't you a funny little one? Of course, you know where we're going. I just told you a moment ago… We're walking to the river to fetch water." She looks down and smiles at him, her brown skin taut against the arches of her brow. "I'm preparing dinner for your father and mother when they return, this evening!"

His father and mother—where have they gone? He is in this body, this young boy, feeling as if he is only seven or eight years old. And he knows her name, Lakshmi… yes, she is his grandmother, his father's mother. He loves being with her, she is so gentle and kind, and she takes him along with her wherever she goes, on her errands in the village and sometimes on adventures such as this into the deep woods, the deep green forest. His feet once again are bare, feeling the cool smooth clay of the path against the toes and the soles of his feet as he walks, carefully, watching the path, looking to avoid any stones or twigs, two steps for every one of hers.

The trail they follow is a narrow footpath, worn smooth by many bare feet such as his and hers, treading it daily, back and forth from the village to the river and beyond, where the next village lies. He knows there is a crossing at the river, a place where it is broad enough and shallow enough to be traversed by walking across the smooth and mossy stones—he has done this before with her. And there is a man there who tends to the crossing, the ford. He has been afraid of that man before, when he went there with Lakshmi, but he will not think of that now, he doesn't even know why he has been afraid of him, only that he is a stranger, and gave him a harsh or questioning look.

He will not think of that now. Now he will walk along and now and then raise his eyes up from the path and see the leaves trace by him, the little blue and orange flowers that sometimes peek from behind the curling branches, the vines and creepers that trail down from high above.

The path is lonely—there are no other people around. They are deep in the forest, the village is far behind, but he does not mind this. The sun is shining high up in the sky and streaming columns of its light sift down through the holes in the canopy of branches and leaves that surround them. Now and then a bird calls out, a squirrel skips away, hearing them approach. He glances over at Lakshmi and sees that she carries a rough wooden pail in her other hand, the hand not holding his own. In his deepest being, he feels calm, still. In his true awareness he can sense that this is a very ancient time, more ancient than he might ever have imagined people such as this walking the earth. In his awareness stepped back from the boy he first senses five thousand years ago, then the realization that this is eight hundred thousand years ago reaches his awareness. Eight hundred thousand years ago… a yellow bird calls out, hesitates on a branch as he comes near, then flits away.

"Will the man at the river be there today?"

Lakshmi looks down at him and smiles.

"There is nothing to be afraid of. Jiva, let me tell you something. The man at the ford is just the same as you and I. I know you are afraid of him, I see how you have watched him before, and I know he can sometimes be harsh with his questions—that's just the way he is. He asks people what their business is, because he lives there and he has taken it upon himself to help people cross the river. And sometimes he asks harshly, that is just the way he is."

They walk along together now in silence. He lets go of her hand because he is tired of holding his own up, lets it drop by his side. The dirt on the path is cool and smooth—he loves the feel of it under his toes. Now and then there are tickling tufts of grass that have grown on the trail, and sometimes he has to lighten his step over patches where sharp pebbles and stones are strewn. He has to look down and watch, to avoid the sharp twigs and stones. He has to watch the undergrowth that creeps in along the sides as well, watch for brierthorns that might reach out and snag him. But this is all part of the fun and makes the walk go by. He does it mostly without thinking, glancing up now and then at the sun and patches of clouds scattered through the bowers across the sky. Now and then some drops of rain drip down, not new rain, drops from earlier this morning when it poured, rain left hanging on the leaves high above him. It surprises him when a drop hits his head or taps him on the nose. And soon enough the trail opens up and he can hear the sound of water streaming over the loose rocks of the crossing just ahead.

The path here changes color from red to tan. Instead of clay packed hard by the weight of many bare feet, the soil has become sandy tan river dirt, muddy in some places where the stream has overflowed its banks. Sticks and branches get in his way, deposited by the river when it last surged across here. He remembers now where his mother and father have gone. His baby sister has been ill, coughing through the night. They have taken her the other direction, to the city where they might give her a spell to take the cough away.

"Lakshmi, will Radhika come back without her coughing?" He looks up to her and sees in her eyes that she will not answer him. Instead, she stares down at him and smiles. This smile is comforting as they approach the bank of the river—in this smile he feels that everything is pulled together, the dirt of the path and the stones in the river that make the river sing its chuckling song, the breeze brushing against the branches of the trees high above, the drops of sunlight that fall down on them through the

45

canopy of leaves, Lakshmi's smile is together with all of that. One thing cannot be separated from another.

But then he dares to take his eyes away from Lakshmi and look across the river, and he sees the man at the crossing and his heart begins knocking, knocking against his chest, a bird that tries to escape its cage. That man is the guardian of the river—he is its master. How can a man master a river? But it is true, for that man with his brooding staring eyes decides who is to cross and who must stay on the opposite shore. He is master and guardian and his sad and doleful look is all-pervading just the same as Lakshmi's smile.

Lakshmi opens her hand again to take his hand in hers, and that is a comfort. Still, he says to her, his voice small and quiet: "Let's not cross. We can stay here, on this side, together."

She doesn't answer him, only holds his hand tighter, as if to say, I am never separate from you, we are together one and all.

He has to take his eyes away from the man who guards the river. That man's feet are crossed, he carries a stick to help him stand upright. His teeth are crooked and brown. His eyes would seek to drown him. Instead, he looks towards the emerald rushes along the shore blowing in the breeze. There are several large river stones strewn amongst the grasses and the sun beats down on them. And then he sees something—what he thought was one of the stones is not. It is something entirely different, not a stone at all. A rabbit, dead, eyes open, ears folded back against its furry skull. Tail nothing more than a fluff of tan fur, the same color as the path, so close he can smell it now, stench of decaying flesh. And around the eyes, black eyes like beads on a doll, flies swarm and dig, dozens of them land and crawl and fly away. Lakshmi sees what he sees and squeezes his hand, pulls him towards the other side of the path and the stones that cross the river. Why, he wants to ask her—why did the rabbit have to die?

Sensing his question and his fear, Lakshmi puts her arm around his shoulders, pulls him close.

"It's okay, Jiva. Even this is part of God."

Even this.

Stood up he stands up—he feels the tug of the denseness inside of him pulling up through arching crescents of leaves into the sky. This part of him that is one with the blanched stones and the hard smooth skin of his grandmother's hand and the black pool of the rabbit's eye ringed with flies, this is lifted through sunlight into starry night. Among the thunder clap of his own unceasing being dark and onrushing torrents of everlasting midnight wrap him in forgotten tenebrous skips of conscious watching, skipping across one instant to the next, trip-wire skipping from one aeon to another, centuries upon centuries crossed as simply as a stream. Across thousands and thousands of years in a lightning strike he finds himself struck and stepped down in another sheath of flesh, another body wrapped around him, another shell with him inside.

Here he stands at a crossroads, three roads come together in a meeting of time and space, a meeting place for him and others like him, he feels the familiar here and also the sense of danger—dread—transported with him from that river crossing thousands upon thousands of years before. The roads form a Y, and at the juncture is a watchtower, no taller than his head, hewn from stones piled one upon another. The tower has served him as a meeting place—he knows, a place where he has met with others of his own kind, in the middle of the night, under full and new and waning moons, though now it is shortly before dusk on a winter afternoon. Sky gray and hanging low, forest shorn of cover. Against the tower someone has placed a crude altar, draped with a faded veronica, veil emblazoned with the face of Christ. To ward off the devil who lingers at the crossroads, to ward against witches such as himself. He can no longer feel safe here—they have turned crossroads into places where bandits and mercenaries wait in shadows to set upon any wayfarers who linger. At certain crossroads they have placed the rotting corpses of criminals and suicides and witches by way of warning—this too may happen to you. And now he remembers; he has a warding of his own to do.

He cannot be sure how he knows this, but he takes the road that angles to his left, to the sinister—that is the way back to the town where he lives. His name . . . he cannot remember his own name at this moment, cannot be sure of exactly who he is, but he knows this is Germany during a time of war, a war that never ends.

For some way the road proceeds through the forest, trees that tower over his head and somehow, he feels, provide him protection, though they may also hide mercenaries waiting to waylay him. In his mind words circulate, words he is using to cast a sphere of protection around him, words he repeats and repeats to the rhythm of his footfalls:

*Hertha, Die Große, die Mutter allen Lebens*
*Die giebert alle*
*Und erneuert ihr Herr die Sonne jeden Tag*
*Wer schenckt sich auf alle Menschen gleichermaßen*

*Wächter des Himmels und des Meeres,*
*Alle Kräfte und Potenzen*
*Sie bringen das Licht zurück, um die Dunkelheit zu vertreiben*
*Nur noch einmal zu uns am sichersten decken mit Ihren Schatten.*

The trees have always been with him, he feels their presence, even though they are dormant in winter, they are alive and he feels their life, their force, towering over him and around him. How many times has he wandered through these woods to gather herbs, flowers, roots, animal bones and skulls, all the elements he needs to prepare the potions and tinctures he sells and gives away to those who need them. To those who have the need of health and potency and God's good favor.

A sudden impulse draws him towards one of the trees—he never ignores the pull of what his gut, his chest, what Spirit tells him. Spirit is leading him to this tree, a whorled and spiraling ancient rowan tree shorn of leaves. He approaches and spreads his arms apart, places the palms of both hands on the trunk as high above his head as he can reach and lets his weight rest against the massive bulk of it. He can feel the energy spiraling off the trunk, extending a field of light around him, shielding him. Once again, silently, he recites his spell, his prayer: *Hertha, Die Große, die Mutter allen Lebens, Die giebert alle, Und erneuert ihr Herr die Sonne jeden Tag...* Silently he chants it, three times, feeling the healing light flow back through his palms and into the trunk of the tree, healing the tree, healing and protecting him. *So soll es sein, so ist es. Amen.*

He steps away from the tree and looks up at its wavering branches towering above him. Not the tallest tree, there are others surrounding it that go far above, but the one that called him. He looks down now, to the forest floor covered with a blanket of decaying leaves, still early enough in winter that they bear the colors they wore when they fell to the ground. The leaves make it harder to see what he is looking for, and most of the herbs are dead by now, but he can still see their remnants—there, near the other side of the tree he just embraced—withered but still useful, a small patch of iris from which he can gather what he needs. He stoops to harvest it, digs into the mulchy soil and pulls up a knot of orris root, securing it in a leathern pouch at his hip. He also removes four twigs from the tree. Spirit never leads him astray—this is exactly what he needs. He can use this to prepare the tincture for the warding.

He returns to the road and walks faster now, there is something going on that draws him back to his shop. Something happening… he needs to be there, and has to remind himself; *nie Eile, nie verziehen.*

Never hurry, never tarry.

At the proper moment everything will happen that is meant to happen. *Nie Eile, nie verziehen.*

Entering the town where he lives in this life, there are people out in the streets still, making good use of the last of the filtering daylight. Winter days are very brief in this northern realm, every moment of sunlight is valuable. A man across the lane heading in the opposite direction watches him, then catches his eye and gestures with a wave of his hand. Not a friendly wave, but an acknowledgment—this is someone he knows. He feels this body, a large body and of great height. Perhaps his own great size is imposing to someone like the man across the road. Still, he feels at home in this body, this sheath of flesh he has found himself in. This is me—him.

He finds his way through the narrow streets without effort. He knows the way here, one more turn around an angled corner and his shop is before him. The front door is unlatched. Someone is already within—she steps towards him and greets him with arms wrapped around his shoulders, reaching up to embrace his great mass.

"Sibyl." The name comes easily to him—he feels a surge of joy seeing her face. Her eyes are a tawny brown blending towards green. Her hair light red tending towards blond and brown together. Her left eye smaller than her right, tighter, giving off a certain glimmer of light. Her arms around him are conveying fear, holding him close as if to shield him, as if her own small body could cover his huge mass.

"They're coming for you."

"I know. Sooner or later—I have felt it."

"They're coming today, this afternoon." She releases him and takes a step back from him, looks him in the eye. Her dark blue gown is clasped at the breast by a silver medallion covered in jewels. Her hair is loose, draped upon her shoulders—not the tightly bound hair of a town matron, nor the hair covered by the bonnet of a maiden—hers is the loose unbound hair of a witch. "Astrid is at the Wine Market Square, and they have the boot on her. Confessing. She's talking, naming names—her sister, her daughter, you, me and Jutta."

He knew, the dread he felt at the crossroads. The warding spell, the orris root.

"Here—help me prepare a sachet."

He hands her the orris root from his pouch. She knows what to do, takes it across the large open room to the walnut table that dominates the center of the shop. This is where he prepares the tinctures, the healing herbs and remedies he sells and dispenses from this apothecary. He looks around the shop and sees—remembers—that he is a very prosperous member of the merchant class in this seventeenth century town. Farmers, burghers, even knights and princes have come to him for his perfumes, powders and ointments, all prepared according to the ancient way of plant lore, passed down by those who have practiced the Craft.

"We'll do the Rowan Cross Spell—we don't have time for anything more than this."

Sibyl knows what to do, she has helped him prepare sachets and tinctures hundreds of times before. Sibyl and Astrid and Jutta help him prepare these and take them out to peasants and townswomen, villagers all around the land. Those who need help with birthing, with conceiving, with warding and with healing. With harvesting crops and sowing, with spells cast against them and with limbs that grow askew. With love affairs and blessings before death—though the church may also provide its care, the common people and those whose power spreads far and wide all seek the help of forces and powers of the earth itself.

While Sibyl gathers the elements for the tincture, he takes a sword he keeps for defense and hangs it above the front door of the shop – ties it with a rope and lets it dangle in front of the door. The iron in the sword he knows will disrupt any spells cast towards him in a more powerful way than using the sword with his own hand. If they are coming for him, they wouldn't dare come with less than four or five men to overtake him; as large as he is, the power he casts out through his mind and conjuring is stronger than his body will ever be. Next, he hammers three nails (all three taken from a coffin) into the door, one above, two below, the triangle of iron jamming any negative powers sent his way. Then, to seal it, he draws his black-hilted steel knife, his athame, and stands facing the east, slightly askew from the front entrance of the shop. He stoops and traces a deosil clockwise circle with the knife point into the stone step leading from the threshold. Within the circle, he traces a pentagram, with the point of the star facing out. And within the pentagram, he incises the name *Gadreel* using the old Theban symbols:

ฦʃฤๅๅๅๆฦฦฦ

That done, he goes back inside and retrieves from one of the many glass-topped cases and cabinets that surround the large main room, a heavy glass bottle lined with lead.

"Is it ready?" he asks her.

"Almost. I need orris root, and the essence."

He hands her the bottle of essence, then pulls the root from his leathern pouch, placing it on the board. With his athame, he slices a thin sliver of the root and chops it into fine pieces. Sibyl sweeps the slices of root with her hand into a mortar and grounds it into a fine powder with the pestle. Once the root is ground up, she adds it to the other elements of the sachet.

"We have everything—powdered orris root, lavender and patchouli, powdered cloves and pimento, pulverized sandalwood. Now the essence."

She has placed all of these elements in a silver bowl. He takes the leaded glass bottle and pours just a couple of drops of the musk essence into the bowl, then reseals the bottle. Sibyl stirs the mixture together, then scoops it into a white cloth satchel. Tying the cloth with red ribbon, she says, *"Ich binde Sie in Hertha Namen."*

She tries to hand it to him, but he will not take it.

"It's for you. You need to go far away from here, and it will protect you. Now the crosses."

He takes the twigs he had gathered from that tree and ties two of them together with the red ribbon, then ties the other two together, closing his eyes and chanting these words, sending the Light into them:

*By this cross of rowan*
*I forbid all adverse and hostile forces*
*Entry to this house and home*
*I forbid you flesh and blood, body and soul.*
*I sternly forbid you entrance to mind, fears,*
*And strengths until you have traversed every*
*Hill and dale, struggled through every stream*
*And river, counted every grain of sand on every*
*Shore, and enumerated every star within the*
*Night sky!*

With the ribbon, he ties the cross around her neck, placing it gently above the silver clasp between her breasts.

*About thy neck this cross I place,*
*Cross of quickbeam, cross of grace;*
*May it safely guard thy way*

*And keep thee safely night and day.*
*Heed this charm, attend to me;*
*As my word, so mote it be!*

Then he has her tie the other rowan cross with red ribbon around his own neck, saying the words again charged with Light:

*Über deinen Hals dieses Kreuz Ich Ort,*
*Kreuz von Eberesche, kreuz der Gnade,*
*Möge es sicher bewachen deine Weg*
*Und halten dich sicher Tag und Nacht*
*Beachten Sie diesen Charme, kümmern sich um mich,*
*Als mein Wort, so soll es sein!*

The dark days are here. That is all he can think of as he looks into her eyes for the very last time. He knows he will not see her again. He draws her close to him and says goodbye. He kisses her on the lips and then once again in the center of her lovely forehead, opening the eye there for her to see all that she may need to see.

"Go now, it is time to go."

"Come with me, we can leave together."

"No, this is my place and my time. If they come for me, so be it. They can only kill me once."

She lays her head upon his great chest and squeezes him. One last time he feels her slight frame encompassed within his arms.

"Go. You know where we said we would meet."

"Yes—I'll see you there soon."

He sends his love and light to her, not with his words, for words are not enough. She releases him and walks out the front of the shop, freely leaving, never to be seen again. Now there is only time to wait. They are coming for him and so be it. At the proper moment everything will happen that is meant to be.

Time slows and accelerates . . . flees and stands still according to his needs. He could leave now too, but he knows, in this moment within the quiet splendor of his empty shop, he knows that he has already lived this moment once before—it has come and gone and now here he is, back again within it, and it must pass as it has always passed, filled with dread and longing, knowing what he is about to endure. The powers he has cultivated in this life have enabled him to step out of it, to see it from a higher plane of vision as it were, at one with the watcher, the higher self that has dropped in here with him, from beyond time, from another place, the self that is his own Self watching over him from above.

Sibyl is not far away yet. He could go with her, couldn't he? He could change the course of these events, could not stand still and wait for them to come. But there is a certainty with which he knows the outcome, a strange sense of detachment watching his own drama unfold—a play with acts and intermissions and an ending that seems inexorable as the seasons passing and the dawning of another day. He traces a circle around his shop, deosil— clockwise—touching certain objects he has come to know and love. The clear glass cabinets filled with vials and bottles offer a dim reflection of his face, his hand raised to touch them. His large head, bearded, hair loose and draped across his hulking shoulders—the men in the town have every right to fear him, and so they do. Perhaps they will not come. He has fortified the shop with powers far beyond his own might, and the cross he wears around his neck divides the world of vision from the world of light. *Kreuz von Eberesche, kreuz der Gnade…* cross of Grace. He repeats the spell silently to himself, then reminds himself—*Ich bin in der Gnade, nicht unter dem Gesetz.*

I am under Grace, not under Law.

Sibyl will be beyond the chapel now, on the road to Nordlingen, across the Ries plain. Astrid is being tortured, or perhaps thankfully she has already died. Jutta is away from town—he had already told her to leave, yesterday or the day before. He told her to go to the farm of their friends the Gebhardts where she will be safe and protected. So, he thinks, if two of us are to die, two of us will survive.

He hears a knock on the door, and goes to look. But it is only the wind clashing the sword against the threshold. The light outside has dimmed, there are no more shadows to be seen. He turns his back on the door and pronounces the Rowan cross spell once more. *Über deinen Hals dieses Kreuz Ich Ort, cross of quickbeam, cross of Grace, Möge es sicher bewachen deine Weg, and keep thee safely night and day—*

Horses' hoofbeats… clamoring and shouting, armor and drunken talk. They have come, not in stealth, but in numbers, as they would need. He turns and faces them, watches through the open doorway—he will not hide. They pull up the horses and dismount short of his shop, fearing an attack from within. Five of them, maybe six. He knows who they are—Jörg Gottlieb, Johannes Engler of course, Hermann Dornhauser, two or three others he cannot see well enough to make out. All of them prosperous civic leaders, aldermen, jealous of his own wealth and the way he has made it, the powers and forces he knows how to use.

"Tomas, haben wir für Sie kommen."

We have come for you.

"Come with us now to the Wine Market square—come peacefully and there will be no trouble. Your sinister friend Astrid has confessed and accused you of seducing her and baptizing her as a witch."

He reminds himself, *Ich bin in der Gnade, nicht unter dem Gesetz.*

Under Grace, not under Law.

His silence enrages them. He will not offer a response.

Engler of course is leading them—Engler stares directly at him and points. *"Erfassen ihn!"*

All six of them charge him at once, rushing through the threshold, past the sword and pentagram, past the barrier he erected. He stands fast, draws the athame and plunges it into the gut of Hermann Dornhauser, the first to launch himself upon him. Three more of them crash against him, waves of surf on a rock. Two more are past him into the shop. He sheds one of them and swings his massive arm,

striking someone's head with his elbow, knocking him to
the floor. One of them goes for his knees, his legs.
Another man leaps on him from behind, pulling him
down. And they are upon him, three of them landing
blows. In the soft round mountain of his gut he feels a
blade being plunged, driven up under his ribs. He lashes
out with both arms, knocking one of them aside, kicks one
in the mouth, sending him flying. Even as he casts aside
one or two of them, two more are upon him, pounding
him with their fists, bludgeoning his head, his chest,
stabbing him with knives. Two or three times he has been
punctured, torso bleeding. From behind him and above,
he hears the sound of shattering glass. His beloved
cabinets are being destroyed, they don't care about the
philters and tinctures, they want the bottles they can sell,
they want the red satin linings on the shelves.

He swings his arms and lashes out with his legs, making
solid contact again, but it is not enough. The spells have
not worked this time, there are too many of them at once,
they would have to come with five or six against him, they
have been wanting to do this for a very long time, and
now it is here, he knows it, what he had been dreading
once the first of the fearful ones, the envious ones, started
accusing him and his familiars of brewing storms, causing
a frail infant to become sick and die. From there it had
been an easy leap to accusations of boiling babies, stealing
an impotent husband's seed, pact-making, seduction, sex
with the Devil. Those they had tried to help with their
herbs and remedies started wondering whether they hadn't

been poisoned instead. The farm animal whose milk ran dry—perhaps that milk had been suckled away by those odd ones who gathered at the crossroads and spoke in weird rhymes. Perhaps Jutta the midwife had caused more children to die than be delivered. Nearly half the infants perished… had the old crone coveted their youthful vigor, dug up their corpses and boiled their tender feet?

He feels himself weakening, he is bleeding from beneath his ribs. His gut is large enough that they have not even come close to an internal organ with their blades, but he is losing blood. He shuts his eyes once to gather himself—he must get up off the ground. And in that moment, he feels a blow to the head, not a fist, something heavy, solid, metal, and his eyes stay closed a moment or two. He hears them ransacking the cabinets, smashing the glass. One of them has brought rope and is binding his feet. Another ties his hands and then they are dragging him out of the shop, down the step and into the street—tying him to one of the horses and dragging him feet first, back on the muddy road, to the Wine Market Square in the center of town.

A crowd follows them, shouting, throwing food at him, shouting his name: "Tomas… Tomas… *Hexe, Hexe, ihn zu töten!*"

"Kill him!"

His head bounces on the cobblestone streets near the square—he can hear the crowd that has gathered now to watch the torture, the interrogations, drawn by lurid curiosity, the spectacle of watching a public execution unfold. It is like a festival, a holiday. They draw up to the stand where Astrid is being interrogated—tortured. His body is covered with bruises from being dragged, and as they unbind him, one of the men kicks him in the kidneys, adding one more.

They hoist him to his feet. It takes three of them to do it, his body a dead weight, his ankles still bound with rope. He can see that Astrid has the boot on—the dreaded boot. Her screams fill the air. She doesn't even have the presence of mind to realize he is here.

Now they have seated him on a wooden platform raised in the center of the square, and of course there he is, presiding over this cruelty, the magistrate. In his weakened semi-coherent state, he cannot remember the man's name… but he knows who he is, the one who does the mayor's bidding, anytime the council needs to have something thwarted or someone put under control. Yes, Fredericus, that is his name, it comes to him now— Fredericus Daul.

"So," he says to his accuser, "you came for me with six men."

Daul stares at him and waits to reply, lets him hear Astrid moaning, lets him hear the crowd calling for him to die.

"Tomas Uhlricht, you have been accused of sorcery and incantation, using strange herbs for casting spells, seduction and adultery and incestuous intercourse. You have been accused by the woman here of luring her to have intercourse with the Devil. With leading a witches' coven and luring witches to fly to sabbaths at the Venusberg on Walpurgisnacht and other nights. Of baptizing witches in the name of the Devil. What say you to these charges?"

"You put these words in her mouth. You're using pain to make her talk. Do this enough and she'll say whatever you want her to say."

Astrid, his cousin—did she really tell them they had sex together?

"Do you deny these accusations? Or do you wish to confess?" He points towards another one of the boots they have waiting for him. "Confess and be saved, Tomas. Spare yourself the same agonies she has been putting herself through."

Do they really believe he would say yes to these things? Of course, the priests are here too, making everything official. One of them, Father Paul, begins spouting scripture.

"For the Lord, the God of Israel, saith that he hateth putting away: for one covereth violence with his garment, saith the Lord of hosts: therefore take heed to your spirit, that ye deal not treacherously."

"I've done nothing but heal people and bless their crops and cattle. Astrid is a healer too... she saved three babies from dying this month alone."

"And yet four infants have perished since all Hallows eve." Fredericus gestures for the boot to be brought over. "Haven't you and your coven of witches been digging up graves of infants? Seven graves have been desecrated—

corpses gone—you're using them for bloody sabbaths, aren't you, and the potions you create with these corpses are not for healing. To the contrary—they are for making women weak and leaching the seed out of men. They are for making crops fail—our harvest has been the worst in twenty-seven years, worst since the wars began."

"We heal people—we help them. Ask Margaretha Betz about her baby Anna. Ask Lorenz Dübner."

"Enough! The Devil is wise in the ways of concealment. Father, help relieve him of the Devil's wiles and loosen his tongue."

Father Paul and two of the others bring the boot over. They untie his feet and place it on his left leg—two curved iron plates that slip over his calf and shin, his foot going into a crude leather shoe attached to the end. The leather straps are pulled tight, binding him in.

"Now, speak Tomas," the magistrate says. "This is your chance to confess. Father is here to sanctify you, to bless you with Holy water and rid you of your demons."

"What demons—I am innocent. I help people use the forces of nature and the natural energies that exist through the power of God and the holy Spirit to their benefit!"

"Blasphemy!" Fredericus calls out, and the calls are echoed by the crowd of citizens gathered around them. "In addition to witchcraft and consorting with the Devil, this man is a blasphemer! He calls upon God to justify his evil and sordid acts."

The magistrate gestures towards the boot. "One application."

The priest and another man he does not know—one of the executioners perhaps, who travel from town to town on these witch hunts—pulls the cords taut, and the metal plates press into his calf and shin, compressing them, sending a jolt of pain up the back of his leg and shooting up his spine.

"Speak. May the Devil loosen your tongue and release you."

He feels the tendons at the base of his calf being pulled and stretched, as the muscle is pressed and lifted away from his heel. His head tips back and he lets out a low moan. He hears Astrid sobbing in the distance, at the other end of the platform, and he does speak finally.

"We've done nothing wrong. We use... forces of nature for good."

"That's not what Astrid has said. She said you compelled her to copulate with her—your own cousin. You compelled her to copulate with the Devil and be baptized by him. You sent several others she has named to farms and villages across the plain to harm the cattle and devour suckling infants. You yourself have been digging up graves—admit your sins and you will be saved!"

He can only shake his head no. They have now built a small fire near his feet.

"Father, another application of the blessed boot."

Father Paul and the hangman draw the straps tighter, crushing the shinbone, compressing his calf muscle and pulling it up, up so taut that the tendons connecting it to the Achilles tendon and thence to the heel now snap with a loud *pop* sending another explosion of pain up his spine. And now they also prop his foot and lower leg encased in the metal and leather boot above the fire—further constricting the leather around his ankle and foot, sending shooting pain from there as well, and causing the metal plates to sear their way into his skin. He cannot even hear himself scream—his eyes are closed to the pain, his ears are ringing and he begins to see lights dance before his vision in his head.

"Stop!!" He does hear this voice, loud, calling out from across the way. It is Astrid—he opens his eyes and looks to her. "I have done it all—it was only me! Leave him alone!"

Fredericus laughs. "She cannot bear to see her lover in pain! Never mind—maintain the application Father Paul. We will have our confession."

She is in pain, more pain than his own. How long have they been torturing her? All afternoon? Since morning? He knows there is no stopping it now—they will both end up dying. So, the sooner the better. The part of him that is outside of him has seen this coming for days now, no spell could save him, but perhaps he has been wise enough to spare Sibyl and Jutta.

The iron plates are broiling their way into the flesh of his calf, and the extra heat they apply is grinding his shin, causing it to snap.

"Okay, yes!" He calls out. "I am a witch, I confess. I have used chanting of the ancient Craft, to cast spells and mesmerize." The pain makes it difficult to speak, he has to draw in another breath to pronounce these words. Words that will end up sealing his own fate. "I have called upon the Devil and consorted with him—it was I, Tomas Uhlricht, who caused Astrid to have sex with the Devil and have sex with me!" He tries to give them what they want to hear. The crowd of people lets out a long cry, filled with fury: *"Hexe, hexe."*

They want more, the more lurid details the better. The fire now is worse than the clamping, the heat of the metal splitting his skin, roasting the muscle and bone.

"I have used potions and witches brew to mesmerize."

"Names Tomas—who have you harmed?"

"Miri Schöttle. I seduced her in the name of the Devil, forced her to consort with him."

"Others."

"Marian Eyferle. I poured my seed into her, killing her unborn child." The more lurid he can make this, the sooner they are likely to release him and Astrid from the pain. "I then dug up the grave of her unborn child and ground the bones for my potions. Boiled the flesh for our Sabbath stew."

"Other names—names of other witches you led to ruin."

"There are no others. Only Astrid and me. It was our upbringing, our family, our parents who are dead now. They taught us these things."

"Wrong—Astrid has named others. Jutta Krempel. Sybil Wagner. What of them?"

"They have nothing to do with us. Jutta is a midwife, that is all. Sybil is a nursemaid—they help mothers, help infants being born."

"They have killed babies. Caused mothers' breasts to go dry."

Astrid calls out again. "Yes—they were the ones. They started all of this, not Tomas. They fucked the Devil and sent him babies' flesh!!"

The crowd calls out. "Find them! Kill them!"

He sees what she is trying to do—trying to save him. But he knows it will not work.

"Enough! We will deal with them later." The magistrate signals to Father Paul. "These two have both freely admitted to their sins. There is only one thing left that can save them." He gestures to a pile of straw and elder branches at the end of the platform. "Now Father, having received their confessions, return them to the Lord from which they came and rightfully belong."

The words come to him again, *I am under Grace, not under Law.*

Thankfully, they push his left leg away from the fire. And release his flayed and roasted calf and his shattered shinbone from the boot. The release of the pressure and pulling away of the plates is almost more painful than what he has endured until now.

Bleeding, bruised, burned and broken, they lift him and carry his huge mass to the pyre. They have tied Astrid to a stake and now bind his wrists behind his back and tie his neck to the stake also, his head lolling to one side, he can barely stay upright on his broken and disfigured left leg.

He begins to chant in a voice only loud enough for Astrid to hear:

*Hertha, Die Große, die Mutter allen Lebens*
*Die giebert alle*
*Und erneuert ihr Herr die Sonne jeden Tag*
*Wer schenckt sich auf alle Menschen gleichermaßen*

He can barely get out the words… why have the chants and prayers failed him? Where has their power gone? Astrid says something, barely a whisper. "I couldn't help it. They tortured me."

They have placed more of the elder branches at their feet, more straw.

"I know. It's not your fault." He feels himself being carried away by the pain. "I love you Astrid."

And now the priest is here again, holding aloft a silver crucifix and pronouncing these words, in a voice that's loud enough for all to hear. "Because they have forsaken me and burned incense to other gods, that they might provoke me to anger with all the works of their hands, therefore my wrath shall be kindled against them, and shall not be quenched." Then, signaling to the executioner to light the reeds and straw on fire, he says, "Lord, forgive them their sins and burn up their iniquities in this holy fire. Consume their unholy lust and accept them, sanctified, into your Kingdom." Then, at the top of his lungs, so everyone in the square can hear: "DO YE THIS IN REMEMBRANCE OF ME."

The branches and straw must have been dried and prepared for days in advance, they accept the flame so readily, flaring and dancing at his feet. In a moment, the flame has consumed the branches encircling them and the heat leaps forth from it, scorching his legs and feet.

Sweat pours from his body, soaks his forehead and drips from his brow. He can smell his own flesh burning, closes his eyes and screams. Why have the spells forsaken him? He keeps pronouncing the words still, the only thing that can stave away the pain.

*Wächter des Himmels und des Meeres,*
*Alle Kräfte und Potenzen*
*Sie bringen das Licht zurück, um die Dunkelheit zu vertreiben*
*Nur noch einmal zu uns am sichersten decken mit Ihren Schatten.*

Then, another thought comes to him, as his consciousness begins to separate from his body—*I am under Grace, and not under Law.* He remembers that he can fly. He knows how to lift himself up, beyond the tethers of this earth and his material body. He remembers that he is not only this flesh, he can transcend. "I am under Grace, not under Law. The earth no longer binds me—loosen all tethers and set me free, I raise myself up and fly to Thee."

He feels himself loosening from the body, leaving all the pain behind. He is one who can leave a body, one who can fly. Spirit is the Watcher, who sees yet does not know. Who flies from life to life, from body to body, death to death and birth to birth. He feels himself lifted up, soaring above the Wine Market Square, raised up and exalted. He is leaving that place, lifted up through the low covering of clouds and beyond through a misted azure sky. The sensation of flying is delightful, so light and free—freed from the confines of that body. Free of the pain. He feels himself floating now, drifting along with nowhere in particular to go, through a black and dreamless space.

Flying is easy—arms lift out in front slightly, legs back, head raised up in the direction he wants to go, eyes closed in the darkness, floating, fleeing, carried along by his thoughts, freedom, loosened from the heaviness of the body. His thoughts will carry him wherever he desires to go. Where? His mind is blank for a moment, and then an image, a summer's day, grass below and blouzy blue sky with clouds towering across the horizon. Beneath him is the roof of a ranch-style house and a concrete driveway and three huge trees—he knows this place, his boyhood home from his own life now, Jacob's life, Jacob's house when he was a teenage boy. He spins around tilting his arms to the left and wheeling about just above the tar-shingled roof. It is just as he left it, just as he would imagine, a summer day perhaps after his junior or senior year of high school, a warm hazy feel in the humid air, cars going by on the two-lane road in front of the house. There was always a steady stream of traffic there, not a lot, but another car passing by at about forty miles an hour every ten or fifteen seconds or so. He and his brother would have to dodge these cars to visit his best friend's house in the neighborhood across the road, or if they had knocked a ball there in the midst of one of their baseball games— they played with tennis balls instead of hard baseballs to avoid breaking windows or smashing one of the cars as it sailed by. He aims himself towards the road now, glancing back to see the broad picture window that dominates the living room and the front of the house. He thinks about the inside of the house, and feels himself sinking a bit towards the ground, lowering. He remembers to direct his thought, focus on something higher to make himself rise. He sees one of the huge maple trees in the front yard, the one closest to the ditch beside the road, on the far side of the driveway and focuses on that. Instantly, he begins rising again and heading towards it. The feeling of lifting up is wonderful, free of the earth, free of the body. His thought directs him, sends him sailing straight towards the burgeoning mass of the tree. He glances down at the road and sees that there is a man walking there on the opposite side, looking up at him, watching him in amazement as he soars across the yard towards the tree.

What must that man be thinking? Does he see him as a person flying through the air, or as a spirit—a ghost? He looks at his own arms outstretched before him and sees they are not fully there. They are slightly diaphanous, a vague impression of the tree and ground below him visible through their shimmering form. The man has halted in his tracks as he watches him soar, but he cannot look down at the walker for too long, or he will be drawn there. He returns his focus to the tree again and he is lifted towards it rapidly, gaining speed. Now the tree fills his vision, the branches stretching out as far as he can see, and he realizes he is about to crash into it, there is nothing he can do to avoid it. He thinks, "Rise, rise," to try and lift himself over it, and it seems to work for a moment, but it is not enough. He is heading straight for the tangled branches filled with green foliage. "Rise," he says aloud, but it is too late. He braces himself for the collision, closes his eyes for a second and then feels himself going *through* the first leaves, the bark, the twigs and branches. He doesn't have to avoid it, he can filter straight through!

The branches are the thickest, he feels them tugging at him—at his cells, his molecules—as he passes through them, they have more resistance. The leaves brush at him, tickling wisps of thin layers flicking at his arms, his legs, his gut. More leaves, more branches, it feels like flowing through an irregular mass of tendrils and fingertips snatching at him. Thicker branches now, in the middle of the tree, fewer leaves, the branches slowing him down. Still he passes through them, his body is very light, mostly made of empty space—it is not a real physical body, it is light enough to fly. Leaves and branches clutch at him, but they are not enough to stop him, he soars straight through. And as he emerges at the other side into the open sky again, he looks down to see the man on the road, halted in his tracks, staring at him in wonder.

The distraction of seeing the man again on the ground, just after flowing through the tree, is too much. He feels himself begin to fall to earth… the road is coming towards him. He closes his eyes and braces for an impact. Surely he cannot filter through a road, or the earth itself? With his eyes closed, something even stranger begins to happen. He sees—feels—a dark red layer of energy he is passing through. He feels colors, red, black, yellow, gold, all glowing, pulsing. There are spots, prickling, flickering all over his skin. He tries to open his eyes and cannot. There is only vibrating color, only a fabric or pulsing red and gold flying craft back into those beasts erected sap murmured at the door this is not the earth embrace this is song of tetrarch fabric of time and space as a dead stone wouldn't paper under do it only fluctuating variegating half enough the tumult under his eyes that will not open only feel again to see. He feels it as a fabric washed loose of time it is still and also pulsing it does not go anywhere it is everywhere is terrible to glorious encounter wish with poison want with hundreds of moments in a single million point of space time goes and never went. Eyes closed ears not sounding there is only feeling here only sense of fluid birth space coupled marry animal forth knowledge kept one over swine among them created dark and flashing light he feels himself losing himself there is only thought face hangs feeling here one only here being space seeing time itself and seeing that time is but the filling up of the gaps between these red pulsing gridworks of energetic objects—the relation ever exist tiny distances between them without the gap there would be only ONE and thence no space no time so he feels himself what is the spirit watching self even this dissolving into full free feckless ancient father feeling nothing more. Return the immensity of only being along the fabric of the nothing mind yellow pulsing red pulsing gold and he can let himself go here ragged reach shone obsolescent disembodied space and no time only going between one gold spot and the next in a comfortable spinning entering tyrant spirit cage one with everything and nothing at all the very fabric of space and time so go with it he feels let it open and be one with all in all so thenceforth proceed to trouble and affright him so close to letting go he can rest here forever there is no need to go anywhere when he is every where he is space and time and power and eyes thenceforth possess

And yet

Whence there is a pause there is a knowing and thenceforth remember and divide and part in two between what is and what was and what came before and what is yet in next to be and that five and twenty shifting from pure sense sensation feeling to a thought of here am I is enough to make him re-member do ye this in remembrance of me re-member come together that old idea of a me of him of he

So going forth he goes and knows that there is he and there is this other red and gold existing space and he emerges from it and in his sense direction of thought of one place to another time emerges forth again and one instant goes into the next and there is him and he is separate from all other

Thenceforth his direction of thought directs him remembers him to where he was meant to be he feels himself pulling together from the pulsing fabric of red and gold and feels a pounding in the top of his head a pulsing pounding nauseating reeling as he slips away in toiling sense of coming together into something such as a body again and sure enough here he is eyes open head throbbing lying flat on his back in a kind of chamber like a sarcophagus staring up eyes open once again at a warm gentle light massaging his face and eyes.

He feels himself inside a body once again—feels his right arm buzzing, tingling with a dense vibration pulsing up and down. Feels his heartbeat heavy thumping inside his chest, double-beating, feeling each bump of each contraction and release, as if it might just as well stop again between each electrical jolt that makes it pound like a drum in his neck and his chest. As if some small furtive animal is jumping around inside him. He feels also now a tingling wet feeling at the top of his skull and a cold frozen almost burning electricity along his toes and ankles and balls of his feet. Eyes close and open again. That soft light, he realizes, is sending him heat as well, warming him—it is designed to do so. And now he notices that the sides, the walls as it were, of the sarcophagus are slowly lowering themselves, and the hard bed or platform he is lying on is raising itself up a bit, bringing him closer to the light.

Eyes close, warm light bathing him, lifting him out of the darkness. A woman's voice.

"Asar."

The touch of someone's hand on his tingling right arm, tugging at him gently.

"Asar, this will not hurt, but remain still for a few moments. I will remove your bandages, and you may feel it pulling on you. You may feel cold for a few minutes."

He opens his eyes and sees a woman's face, with dark hair arranged within a kind of helmet, a device she is wearing. She lifts something away from his own face—a mask, shining, fashioned of gold. And now she is tugging on strips of fabric, pulling them away from his neck and shoulders, gently removing them from his skin. He feels wet and cold, can still feel that strange small animal jumping in his chest and neck, heartbeat thumping against his ribs. Feet tingling and cold as two blocks of ice. Now another young woman appears and has started removing strips of fabric from his mid-section, exposing his navel and his groin.

The light from the lamps is pouring over him, heating his cold lifeless blue skin, bringing the circulation back. One of the women tears something away from his leg too fast and the pull of it hurts him, sends a jolt of pain up his spine.

"Ah—oww."

"Forgive me Asar. Some are still bound to you more than others." She says this as if he knows what she is doing, as if he has done this before. He tries to raise his head, lifts it a few centimeters from the slab he is on, finds he can raise it no further.

"Easy," the first woman says, "lie still. There is no hurry. It will take a few minutes for your body temperature to come up. And until then you should remain here and let the crystal refresh your cells. They have been dormant for eighteen years."

Eighteen years… what is this place?

He closes his eyes again and lets the warmth of the light pour over him. He remembers now, it is coming back to him. The crystals are in the lamps above him—the light they send forth has been refracted within their crystalline structure to a high level of purity which can penetrate the cellular and molecular structures of his body to regenerate it, not only to raise the body temperature, but to repair any damage and deterioration that has happened while he was away—while he was dead. He is being brought back to life, and his body was preserved in embalming fluids and bandages to protect it while he was away, in anticipation of his return. He can smell the fluids, that is another function of the light of the crystals—to dissolve the fluids that have been soaking his insides and his vital organs, to wash the fluids away. The smell is a sour chemical smell—an odor combining vinegar and the sickly-sweet scent of meat that has been left to rot. He takes his mind from it, draws his attention elsewhere. It is too soon to open his eyes, he knows that now, and he can only think of the voice of the woman who spoke to him. He had a glimpse of her when he first looked around the room, a woman of small stature, no more than five feet tall, dark hair, soft green eyes looking at him with compassion. She knew his name, spoke to him as if she had been expecting him, as if she knew him from before… he passed away.

They are still working on him—there is another woman whom he heard but has not seen. The one who pulled his bandages away too quickly. He will keep his eyes closed and let the women work, draw his focus within, centered deep inside him. He lets the remembrance of this place drift toward him and thinks about who he might have been. That name—she called him Asar, can that not also be a woman's name? No, he remembers it now, some of his previous life here coming back to him. He was a priest of the temple, he lived near this place—chanting, always chanting, always hearing the hymns of God in his ears. The music of the temple ringing now he can hear it in remembrance how he would chant and sing. Now perhaps they will take him there again, to his beloved altar stone, to the place where he sang the seventy-seven names of God.

"Asar, lie still. Do not speak. Let the crystals do their work. In a few moments the others will join us for the ceremony."

He keeps his eyes closed, though he wants to look at the woman again. She seems to know him and care for him—is she someone he once loved, or merely an attendant whose task it is to tend to him as he takes form in this body once again? He can feel more of his body tingling, vibrating, that heavy sensation of blood circulating again through the tissues, feels it in his chest and in his gut, tries to keep from thinking of that chemical smell. He feels them pulling bandages away from his forehead, away from his ears, and now he can hear them better, the sounds around him are clear, less muffled. He hears others coming towards him surrounding him and still he resists opening his eyes again.

A man's voice now. "How is he?"

"Doing fine, body temperature rising nicely. He tried to sit up at first, but he is more relaxed now."

"Good—are there any signs of *machtah?*"

"No, I believe everything is functioning as it should, at least at this point. We'll know more after the ceremony."

With eyes closed he must have slept for a while—a moment or two, maybe longer. Time has no form for him, each moment is its own emblem of eternity. Again he tries to open his eyes—he can keep them open a bit longer, blinking and squinting to focus and shield them from the light. Even from his brief view before, he can tell that he is in a different room now, they must have moved him from where he first woke up. The giant crystal light overhead is gone. Instead, the ceiling is high above him here, the space is much bigger, the ceiling arching above him like a dome.

"Lie still, Asar." Her voice again, the first one. "We will begin soon, and that will help you come together."

He had not moved, or maybe he did move and didn't realize it. The body he inhabits still feels very strange to him—heavy, dense, like being tucked inside a huge slab of meat. He can feel his fingers tingling now, warmer than before. His feet still slightly cold. And he can feel a blanket or some kind of garment covering him, helping him warm up. The heat of the light overhead has been replaced now by the huge airy space of this room—it feels familiar to him, he keeps his eyes open longer and sees that it is perhaps the temple they have wheeled him to, the central chamber. He tries to raise himself and finds he can lift his head off the slab enough to see more of the room around him: cream-colored stone adorned with murals depicting the ceremonies and the gods who are worshipped here. He remembers: he spent many hours, days here celebrating in bliss. The displays of light and color and music—the soft lure of the incense, but mostly the music.

He can sense the presence of many people around him, and the presence of the two women—he thinks of them as sisters—one of them who sits at his feet attending, and the other who hovers over him near his face checking something, tugging at something along the side of his brow. And a tone sounds now, the progressive sequence of tones, majestic, unfolding, opening up, one from another. Can he be in the temple he remembered?

There is a roll of drums, strong drumming sending out a wave of sound followed closely by the sound of bells clanging, ringing out and destroying with their discordant shuddering any lingering vibration of death or decay. Horns sounding a clarion call—and the sound of a loud voice shouting out:

"Asar, come forth! I am come to thee—Let thy soul see its body once again. Let thy soul unite itself with the body this day. I am the son who lifteth up my father."

He can feel the women attending him, the one at his head removing more of the bandages, the one at his feet pulling strips of cloth away and wiping his cold feet to clean the fluid from them.

The trumpets sound out the same glorious note five times in quick succession, and the drums roll low and loud again.

"Asar, come forth to day!" The loud voice calls out again, shouting out: "Asar, I have come to thee. I am the herald of his words to thee whose throat stinketh. I restore thee unto life this day with the offerings of all good things. Rise up, then, Asar—I have stricken down thine enemies for thee. I have delivered thee from them."

He can feel a bright light shining on him from above—he can feel the touch of the woman at his face and the one who is seated at his feet, wiping his feet with a warm cloth, so fine it feels as if it has the silken texture of a woman's hair. He can feel the light coming it must be from the crystal in the high dome above him, sending pure energy—pure sound—pure light in the form of crystalline structures that are healing and transforming his body from decay at the level of the cells and even at the level of the molecules within the cells. He can feel the light of this crystal energy as a flood of warmth engulfing him, tingling through him beginning in his right arm and modulating to his left arm and shooting up both legs from his feet where the woman caresses him. He can feel the flood of holy light filter through his solar plexus pulling it taut, lending it strength and flooding as a river up through the gut to his heart. He can hear the bells ringing and the trumpets sound again. He can hear the woman at his feet weeping.

"Come thou to me, Asar." The loud voice of that man, the priest, is closer now, near to his body.

"Hail Asar, thou art born twice! Arise from thy bed and come forth!"

And now he feels something touch him—a rod, a wand—something prodding him at the center of his forehead and the center of his chest, where his heart is faintly beating, followed by a strong jolt of energy—as if he has been stunned by an electrical shock.

"O thou who art called aloud—Asar, come forth! I have delivered thee from pain and suffering that were in trunk, shoulder and leg. I have healed the trunk and fastened the shoulder and made firm the leg. I open for thee thine eyes that thou mayest see with them. O thou who art called aloud—I have given thee thy soul, I have given thee thy strength, I have given thee thine two eyes, I have given thee to day two divine sisters who attend to thee and bring you back to life."

He feels the two women place their hands on him— one on his feet, gently, and the other on his forehead and the center of his chest.

"O thou who art called aloud—open thine eyes and see."

He obeys the command, opens his eyes and sees the one he thinks of as the second woman—not the first one who attended him—looking down upon him. He sees the pulsating light of the crystal high above them in the dome of the temple sending pure golden white light to heal him, feels the light transmuting his form. He sees the priest with the rod, the staff held over his chest, the rod that shocked him, the tip of it still glowing dull orange. And he raises his head to look towards his feet and sees the one there who attends to him, wiping his feet with a cloth of finest linen.

He feels a very strong connection to this beautiful woman, feels life surging through him again. He raises himself up to look at all the people gathered round about him. He blinks his eyes once, twice, and it is all still here.

The priest cries out in his loudest chanting voice:

"O thou who art called aloud, thou the lamented, thou art glorified, thou art raised up. Asar has been raised up by means of all the manifold ceremonies performed for him to day."

Then, all the people encircling him on his death bed call as one: "Hail, Asar, thou art born again!"

He feels his body full of light, feels the muscles in his legs and shoulders tense and taut now full of the tingling of circulating blood. He raises his head further and with eyes still open sits all the way up upon his bier, his deathbed a sanctum of birth once again. The two women who attend to him, he remembers their names now— sisters, the one at his head named Merta and the one who has been wiping clean his feet named Marya.

"Stand forth, rise Asar who art born again!" The priest who has been shouting these words of the ceremony nods to him, signals that it is okay to stand. His feet dangle from the end of the platform—the sister named Marya there nods to him as well.

"It is time, Asar," she says in a quiet voice, eyes downcast. "You may stand now." The one at his head named Merta takes hold of his hand, to steady him. Carefully, he leans forward and places his feet upon the floor—cold floor made of stone warmed only by the light of the crystal in the dome high above. Feet firmly on the floor, he raises himself up and stands, Marya taking his other hand to lead him.

Again, all the many priests and witnesses of the ceremony call out in loud voices amidst the trumpets' clarion call, the beating of drums and bells clanging their toll.

*"Hail, Asar, thou art born again!"*

Marya and Merta then place a robe of finest linen over his shoulders to cover him in his nakedness, lead him forth, across the temple sanctus sanctorum towards a banquet table laden with every manner of food and drink.

Merta speaks to him, pointing to a large round cake with the shape of a cross cut into the top of it. "Eat this, partake of the cake of resurrection. Drink of this wine and eat this meat which has been prepared by the priests in this holy place. They will bring you strength."

The smell of the meat is vaguely repulsive to him, too strong. He tears off a piece of the cake, more like a thick crumbly loaf of bread, warm in his hand, and places it in his mouth. The sensations of eating, chewing, are strange—though the taste of the cake is sweet with a tinge of salt to it. With some effort he swallows and gestures for the cup of wine. Merta hands it to him and he swallows the bitter liquid, washing the cake down.

"Eat more," Marya says. "I know it's not easy at first, but your body needs nourishment. It has lain sleeping all these years."

"Take a bite of the meat." Merta hands him a torn sliver of lamb flesh on the end of a skewer. He places it on his tongue and chews, the strong taste of it making him gag. "Take it down," Merta says. "It will give you strength."

He swallows and takes another long draught of the wine to cover the taste. Too strong, too visceral. Too close to the sensation of being inside his own body once again. Words form and he finds he can have the force to utter them:

"Enough—thanks to both of you."

Marya takes his hand again and leads him towards a giant doorway, the threshold of the temple, the doorway of this chamber which had been his tomb.

Once more the music rises in crescendo—the flutes and strings softly lifting the horns. And once again the priest who conducted his raising up calls out in his loud voice.

"O thou who art called aloud, Asar, thou the lamented, thou art glorified and raised up!"

He scans the room and lifts his arm as a way of saluting them, all those who gathered to see him come forth again into this world. Then he turns and leaves the temple with

Merta leading the way and Marya holding him by the wrist for support. Through a long corridor they walk, slowly, passing door after door. They are inside, he feels, a huge building, the weight of it massive. The hallway seems to go on forever, but perhaps it is only his own weakness as he walks that makes it feel this way. Then Merta waves her hand and one of the doors slides open. She enters the room and Marya leads him in as well. Merta points to a bed at one end of the dim room.

"Lie down and rest if you wish. It will take some time for your strength to gather."

Marya leads him to the pallet. "We will bring you anything you desire—if you want more food or drink, just say so."

"Water… very thirsty," he says, and gingerly lowers himself to sit at the end of the bed.

"Of course." Merta pours a glass of water from a porcelain pitcher and hands it to him. "I will leave you now." She glances at Marya with a look that he can only decipher as envy, goes out.

With Merta gone, Marya touches him now on the face for the first time.

"You were away so long. I was beginning to wonder if you would ever come back."

"It feels as if I have been gone forever." He allows himself to look into her eyes, for the first time. "How long was I away?"

Even as he asks the question, he remembers what she is about to say. She told him this before.

"Eighteen years. Long enough... that I considered being with another." She must have been his wife. Still is his wife. And Merta is her sister. "I knew you would come back—the priests foretold it. And you have done so before."

"Still, never away this long—I feel as if this body is not my own. As if I don't belong here."

"Lie down and rest, and I will lie with you."

He does as she asks, lies upon the cool linen sheets and rests his head on a pillow that accepts it and cushions it in a way that is so comforting his eyes instantly close. His consciousness drops away and a part of him expects to leave this place behind once more, but there is a strong pull here, an attachment to this body that has been strung in place by the ceremony he just endured, by the light pouring down on him in the temple and the rod of the High Priest. He allows himself to drift off into sleep for a moment, maybe longer. What comfort there is in letting himself go into nothingness for a moment... cool blank darkness.

Perhaps he has slept for three minutes or perhaps it has been three hours, he cannot tell. The next thing he feels is the touch of Marya's hand on his chest, then lower, along the taut flank of his waist, just beneath his ribs. Instinctively, he puts his arms around her and pulls her close to him. She responds by pressing her lips against his and reaching her hand lower still. His body feels leaden and weary and yet also full of life, the sensations of her hands and lips and breasts pressed close to him sending tingling charges through nerve endings that have been dead to the world for years upon years. An electrical glow seems to engulf them, a halo of auric mystic light. She rolls onto her back and he climbs on top of her and joins himself to her. They have been separated too long. Plunging inside her feels as if he is joining with a long-lost part of himself, another piece of him he must have to make himself whole. Another layer of his soul that has been needlessly stripped away. She raises up to meet him, and they combine their essences together light upon light, flesh within flesh. This is why—this is the reason for being. To join with another soul in such a manner that two become one. To separate from the One and find it in another again. To know what it is to be alone and suddenly learn how separateness can be transmuted into eternal exultation and glory. To send forth and release into the great void the sum and substance of his being. To cry out and hear the echo of his cry in the blank awareness of the other, mirror of himself, mountainside and valley low. When it is over, he rolls aside and lies there listening to her breathe. When it is finished, he keeps his eyes closed and feels her warm legs against his own. He sees a violet circle of light within his inward vision and tries to sink down into it. To no avail. He tries to see if he can leave this body once more, to no avail. He feels himself very much rooted here, in this place, whether it is simply because of the sex or the ceremony which centered his soul upon this form and raised the body up, he cannot be sure. But he feels as if for the very first time this is the body in which his spirit, his everlasting conscious awareness, has become entrapped.

He cannot lie here any longer—he has been lying still for years and years. He sits up slowly, his body stiff and muscles aching. The backs of his hamstrings sore. She is still sleeping beside him. Gently tossing the sheets aside he rises from the bed and pulls the linen robe over his shoulders. There must be a way to go outside. The sun is slanting lower through the narrow window but there is still plenty of daylight left. To the right of the window is what looks to be another door. He approaches it and holds his hand towards it, the same way the other woman did as she left the room. Immediately it slides open, allowing him to step through to a kind of covered porch surrounded by columns. As soon as he is far enough through the threshold, the door slides shut behind him. Spread out before him is a vast tropical garden surrounded on two sides by the columned portico of the temple. The marble columns of the temple gleaming white in the late afternoon sun and the friezes that line the galleries above them painted in vivid, almost garish colors. He takes in this scene of swaying palm trees and birds darting here and there and allows himself to simply breathe in the fresh ocean air. Out across the vast horizon is the water, the ocean that surrounds this island continent, gleaming silver, gold and turquoise in the distance.

Steps lead down from the portico to the garden below. He follows them and soon he is among the palm trees, walking in bare feet on a sandy path that leads to the water. Yes, he remembers that all roads, all paths lead to water in this place. The path skirts the edges of a lagoon, and so he sheds his robe and steps from the sand into the water, so warm it is almost like a bath. He moves forward and submerges himself in the water, buoyant salt water, fed to this lagoon from the sea. He closes his eyes and swims breast stroke into the deep soothing tide, letting the water support him, washing his body clean and releasing the tension from his limbs. He opens his eyes once more and swims towards what he thinks of as the mouth of the lagoon, a large low bridge where the path crosses over to the shore of the opposite side.

Under the bridge he swims and there at the mouth of the lagoon he stops and allows himself to float and take in a fantastic view, something he never thought he would see again. Across the space of an open bay flashing with scintillae of early evening sun, rising from the water the golden rooftops of the most magnificent city he has ever been privileged to see. Buildings and columns white and low to the ground, similar to the temple he was just in, but so perfect in their proportion, all of them rectangles of shining white light topped with angular scaffolds of gold. He can see that the opposite shore of the bay leads into a series of canals that intersect and lace the city with passageways for ships and all manner of watercraft to transport people and goods and animals and savory foodstuffs of every variety brought here from lands near and far. Even from this distance he can feel the city thrumming with the activity of millions, and yet it does not feel crowded. There is grace and proportion in every aspect of this place, as if a heavenly hand has guided the planning of it. Flying machines hover and glide through the skies above—strange golden white aircraft that linger over a particular building, maybe picking up a passenger or depositing something there, then in a quick instant darting away into the sky. They flit about like hummingbirds sampling nectar from a garden. And the city *is* a garden, lined with palm trees and the scent of hibiscus mixed with salt ocean air. He raises his eyes above the aspect of this burgeoning city to a broad plateau that rises up beyond it. Here, surmounting the plateau, is a sight so magnificent, it takes him a moment to register what he is seeing. The plateau must rise some two hundred or three hundred feet above the city below—it is hard for him to judge the heights and distances—and rising from the plateau is a pyramid of gleaming white marble fronted by a golden tabernacle that serves as the entrance to the holy of holies. This pyramid is so vast his eyes have to readjust to take in the scale of it. It must be seventy stories tall, a thousand feet across at the base. A broad marble stairway leads up from the city below to the plateau and thence to the golden tabernacle. This is the center of the earth, the omphalos, navel of the civilized world, and he remembers now the name of this city, this place: *Atlan.*

He allows himself to float there in the water entranced by the vision of the giant pyramid and the vast city at its feet. Beyond the pyramid is the magnificent backdrop of high snow-covered mountain peaks, rising up from the tropical plain of the coast. Perhaps this is his real home, the place where his spirit first came to dwell in the physical plane. He tries to think of a time, a date for this existence and the thought that comes to mind is 57,000 years ago— and this thought, the idea of a time before *now*—before what?—causes a glimpse of another life, another mountain top to enter his head. A glimpse of himself hiking up a rocky path to the wind-blown plateau above that village in the south of France where he labored to assemble a work of art that might somehow capture the exalted feeling of this sacred place. An image of the wind blowing curtains of sheer metallic fabric across the face of the sun comes to him—another place, another life—but which one is really him? Which one is real, and which is a dream? He tries to project himself into the vision of that other place, the mountain top with the shuddering expanse of fabric draped across it, and finds that he cannot go there, cannot move his awareness beyond the confines of his head, the vault of his skull in this body here where he has become rooted, floating on the tranquil salt water of the lagoon. That other place is only a shred of a dream that is fading away into the receding shadows of his memory moment by moment. This is where he lives—Atlan is his home now.

The thought is comforting to him. He doesn't need to escape the body and travel in those other, astral planes. Why leave? This bay, this city, this water warm as a bath, the bed with Marya in it waiting for him to return, who could want more than this? He rubs his hand along the taut muscles of his upper arm and shoulder. This body is a suitable home for his spirit, strong, young and filled with the rejuvenating light of the crystal. He can live here as long as he likes, enjoying every sensory pleasure he could ever hope to want. Joining with Marya night and day, her body waiting for him, ever willing. The warm sun bronzing his skin, the cakes and sweetmeats and wine all his for the asking. He closes his eyes and basks in the recalcitrant silver gold light of the setting sun. In contrast to this moment, this place, that other life, the life of that artist in that fragment of a dream—what was his name? he cannot recall—the life of that artist and the people of that time seems coarse and dull, savage in its regrettable feeling of lack, always striving for satisfaction and not knowing how to receive it.

He opens his eyes again and stares at the looming white mass of the pyramid. There is a double meaning to it. Instinctively, he knows what it is for—it is the source of all power. It is the center of the world grid, the navel of the earth, drawing up from the depths of the planet all the energy needed to power the crystals in the temple he was just in, and the lights of the city and the watercraft in the harbors and airships floating in the sky above. It is the center of an immense toroidal vortex of energy spiraling out of the earth and into the atmosphere above, magnetically drawing in and sending forth a field of invisible force that is strong enough to surge power through every living being within the city and the far reaches of the fields and mountainsides beyond. It is this, and also something more. As he looks at it, he sees that the pyramid is also a portal, a gateway to other dimensions, where souls such as his own can come and go, where he only recently did pass through to resurrect here once more. Gazing at the vast marble white face of the pyramid makes it shimmer, glisten and glow. The golden tabernacle opens the door to the holy of holies. Spikes of green and silver sunlight leap into the sky above. The form of it dazzles and shifts, fades in and out of view. It is a doorway and that door can slip open just as easily as the doors that slide aside in that room where Marya waits. It is a gateway to a yawning chasm of darkness and light it is a spinning angular momentum of forces that conspire and unite to tear a hole in the fabric of this time. That is why the pyramid can be two things at once—the power generated by the toroidal vortex can be used by the city and the airships and watercraft and anything within dozens of miles of here but also there is so much energy surging through the vortex that it can be used to puncture the fabric of the local space-time. The pyramid and the city were built here for a reason: this place is one of the twelve key nodes on the grid of earth energy, and the giant pyramid only serves to amplify the energy that has always flowed through here. He remembers this now—how to do it. He stares at the gleaming gold tip of the pyramid, a thousand feet above him, where all of the spiraling energies of the earth converge in a single point and switch their polarity to the opposite direction, spiraling up and out in a giant twisting toroid of light. He closes his eyes now and projects his consciousness out through the center of his forehead in the direction of the tip of the pyramid merging his conscious awareness with the golden juncture of all power seeing a sphere of slashing bronze light in his inner vision conceal splendor singing months nothing like the flute beloved raising octaves now to amaranth magenta preparatory rising lay thee hold of thy inner vision and rising bring it from gold and green through turquoise azure light to raise and bring it in his inner vision between the eyes to rich light violet magenta the velocity blinking God light through his inner vision linking his one pure self with the invitation of singularity at the very tip of the glancing called the endless form aligning too much with it his inborn self drawing to the very depth of pathetic wreath of power arising from the tip of the swirling light achieving escape velocity which allows his awareness not to go above nor beyond but to puncture and release itself from this stratum of physical alignment of perception bursting itself through puncturing a plastic bag of entanglement which his consciousness has been wrapped in here and rushing out through the open flittering ends of that filament of time and space and into a years' wide rebellion of open emptiness and vastness beyond the void feeling his self expanding expanding going on and on forever so terrible to lose himself and let go and also so much a freedom from the limitation of form he feels himself borne along by a wind bright astonishing in its retreating task of velocity to carry him along through a black open emptiness and establish him in another element of stinging bright atmosphere of wrought iron hardened light this new place is an intermediary he feels a place in between forms between lives the life he just left in Atlan (why again did he leave it?) and whatever other life he will come again to next this place is not so much a place as a dimension—a freedom from space time and form {do ye this in remembrance of me} he is not standing here or being here as he would in other lives on a more physically defined planet standing with his feet rooted to the earth or even floating in a liquid element such as water—here he is not standing or walking or resting rooted to the ground, here he is flowing surging coming going carried on by the seven hundred mile an hour wind his body gone his mind moving faster than sound has become a sound, a resonating chord harmonic echoing among other spirit sounds that are flowing on this wind along with him. He is on another planet here and also in another dimension—he has lost his human form he has dropped it like a plastic wrapper that was closing him in it had felt good again for a few hours to be wrapped up in that meat and stiff bone casing to slow himself down and stand still and limit himself to a slow droning single-minded filter of awareness but now having dropped the wrapper and unleashed his own mindful awareness out into the vast expanse and swiftness of the ammoniac sky and hydrogen wind life does not have to have a body to exist life is conscious awareness and exists in myriads of forms and he has simply pierced the veil of lower dimension and expanded into a higher vibratory state that is life unconfined vibrations singing on a wave of super sonic wind this world he is in now is colored green and ochre turquoise orange blue, white hydrogen rich ammoniac sharp tint of piercing sulphuric acid lifting where the temperature pushes up to higher layers this is an interlife dimension and also another space another place another planet where spirits spin as flowing winds for times unknown time moves both forwards and backwards here past and future tangled up and free this is a planet filled with spirit winds and rings of glowing ice that lace it with shadows this he knows in that other world he came from as saturn bull of the sky chronos keeper of time Seb Keb Chronos Kaiwan Repa Chiun Rephan Satre rings and glory star of might star of god in the night sol invictus death of the sun returning governor of time and space yet here there is no time and space is freely flowing unfettered and unbound were he to realize that is why the retreat and failure seems to symbolize from whence he came as here it is the freedom from limit failure and form freedom from bounteous tasting hearing door to perception opened up to enunciate still haunted the land no more with violence sailor on the wind and of the wind and he is the wind for even the wind is alive is pure Spirit flowing free discovered uncovered a connected flowering flowing breath of Spirit pure sound leaving chords of tones overflowing one through another through the pressurized ammoniac skies perfecting trembling saviour desire country mirroring thoughts and emotions like unto shadows across the frozen crystalline sky thoughts are feelings too emotions are Spirit energies flowing winds that gather and release and cast their shadows in this dimension where solid bodies don't exist he is in this planet saturn and of it and also it is a separate dimension from the want and limitation he has known in the lives in between the pouring in of his unlived spirit into bodies encasements driven down into human forms with arms and legs and hip bones shoulder blades and eye balls to witness through plastic wrapper to conduct his feeling tension tortions through all gone away here his spirit is wider than a continent and faster than a vermillion knotted foam unfurled long-armed unbound the Spirit has no measure no time so static borrowed space and those earth-bound versions of himself look up in the night and see the semblance of this dimension in time-space lit up like a candle in the ravaging silent tempering blue black dawn given the words she longs to hear driven energies in motion are the spirit winds of saturn thoughts more real than birds in flight sadness joy and bittersweet devotion cast their shadows cross the song of stranger perishing dreamtime loveliest of tightening honour shall hold the humble in spirit pervading from that day and all the time going forward even as it retreats joy casting shadows of cimarron and gold, silver blue and white sadness casting shadows of crimson bloody deep and still and bittersweet devotion known also as love driving shadows from high above compact visible tangible sensible song that is signing long and nigh] his spirit [is this and ever shall be witness of this and always shall carry this with him whenever and wherever it shall draw itself within a slowed down tempered tempted into one physical stillness of bodily form these emotion thoughts filtered through as colors and chords resounding through all the atoms of his being each flowing through him as expressions of the highest dimensions drowned into a table tangible function of all that dwell in the land]; eternities have passed and will pass once he flooded into this sphere of whirling mass and yet this is only a momentary pause between one day life year and the next |he has let go of himself to be released into a higher vibrating octave on this planet but remembrance brings him back to gather himself into a smaller lower tighter funnel of wind tightening spiral of filaments of thought {do ye this in remembrance of me} remembrance of whom? That person that other one who journeys from one life to another, fights battles with various versions of himself having forgotten that everyother is another mirror motion of his only single-eyed unitary soul. That entity that goes about longing for another chance to bring forth beauty unto the world, expressing himself in so many ways that he cannot help but one day get it right. Remembrance of being drawn down into a slow motion unfolding of his multi-faceted gemstone thistle soul, where thoughts and emotions are invisible and only their outer casings can be felt and seen and known. There he longs to be again—slowed down and drawn within to a single stillpoint of knowing. And as every thought feeling emotion here comes forth in the very selfsame instant, so be it, so it is, Amen.

In the living room of a ranch house in the burgeoning suburbs of a Midwestern city on the solid firm ground of Earth he finds himself standing holding a tinkling tumbler of gin laced with carbonated water and garnished with a lime, wearing a pair of tight high-waisted slacks, dress shirt and collar that scrapes beneath his chin. Several other people are gathered around what appears to be a large metallic box, silver or gray, depending upon which way the late evening sunlight strikes it. They have summoned him here, it seems, to examine this box. He is having trouble getting his bearings so suddenly has he been dropped into this life on Earth by his own instantaneous desiring of it, but it feels to him that this must be a life he lived in the 1950s, though how can that be? He lived as a little girl in that era, the little girl that ran across the cornfield and watched her father die in the airplane that crashed to the ground. How can it be? He shakes his head, takes a sip of the drink to clear away the cobwebs and focus, regain awareness of who he is and what he is doing here in this moment, crystalline moment stolen away from the interstices of time.

Yes, they have called him here, to tell them what is wrong with this box.

One of them, a slender gorgeous woman with dark hair flipped out at the ends in the form of a helmet to frame her slightly angular features, approaches and takes him by the hand. Is he related to her in some way? He feels a strong attraction flowing from her, as she opens her mouth to speak.

"This box is haunted. What can we do with it?"

The look she gives him is a pleading urgent request to make this thing go away. The others stare at him as well— a family, the woman's husband, a boy maybe ten or eleven years old. They may be his relatives, the woman a cousin of his perhaps. She lets go of his hand with a lingering expectancy that propels him towards the box. He is drawn towards it. The box appears entirely out of place in this living room, furnished as it is in mid-century modern simplicity. He has no idea how such a thing would have gotten here—it is as foreign to the scene as he himself feels, utterly incongruous. Still, he can feel the urgency of the family calling him to take some kind of action.

"It's haunted," the husband says. "There are ghosts in it." And what he has left unsaid is the request to make it go away—these people are frightened.

He steps towards it. The box doesn't frighten him, only evokes a mild curiosity that such an unusual object could appear within this living room, as if it were deposited here from outer space, much the same way he has been. The box is about three feet on a side, perfectly square, a metallic cube that looks as if it could be a shipping container for some kind of exotic, fragile work of art. Now that he has stepped closer to it, he sees that the top face of the box is etched with a series of peculiar symbols, scimitar shapes and curling insignia that must be some kind of alien alphabet unlike anything he has ever seen. The sight of these characters sends a chill up his spine. This object is utterly foreign to this time and place—it has come from somewhere just as strange as he has. An electrical chill is making his hair stand on end. As he steps closer, the others stand back in fear. He is not afraid of it, but the sense of another being here is very strong, and that is what is making his hair stand on end, the sense of another presence—as the man said, the feeling of a ghost watching him just over his shoulder, which makes him glance behind him. There is an electrical current floating around here, a field that surrounds the box. Maybe that is what they are all sensing, an electrical charge that's coming across as the feeling of a spirit. He has the urge to reach towards the box, puts his hand out to touch it, and as he does so he is suddenly overwhelmed by the flooding forward through his arm and up to his forehead the sensation of a dozen or more beings flowing through him, filling his forehead with their presence. As if they are reaching out to him with their forms as well. He feels them flooding forward through him and though his hand has not touched the box, cannot touch it, he is now connected to it, can feel the living presence within it flowing towards and through him, making his head jolt back. He immediately thinks of these beings as aliens, from another planet, beings so highly advanced and foreign to this place that they must be from a distant star and planet. There are no voices he can hear, no sound, but he can understand from a feeling of pure thought-form these impressions upon his conscious thinking:

"We are here with you always, though you know it not. We are watching over you, though you care not to know it. We are not from another world, we are of this planet. We have been here millions and millions of years."

And now there are no words for what is being communicated, he is only able to see and sense what they are conveying to him within the imagery of his mind, with eyes closed, he sees what they are showing him from a time so long ago he would never have imagined that intelligent beings could have dwelled here on this Earth— as they express it, what he sees is from a time millions of years ago, when a civilization so advanced inhabited this Earth, it makes the technologies of the current era in this living room he is standing in seem like the spears and stone implements of a cave man. They are showing him human beings, not much different from his own form, inhabiting vast crystal cities that glowed with power from the light of the sun, people who lived in such a high state of harmonic resonance with their surroundings that the vibrations of their bodily etheric field enabled them to communicate with one another and with other animals and even plants in much the same way they are communicating with him at this very moment—with thought forms transmitted as energy waves in the form of high-frequency sound. A kind of transcendent music—he pictures it as a form of singing with light. These people are, or were, in that time millions of years ago, thousands of times more advanced even than the people who lived in the pyramid city by the sea. The symbols on the box are the remnants of their civilization's language, from an even earlier time when they once used spoken words. They lived on the land and also beneath the sea. They lived in the sky, as they outgrew the need for their bodies. They shed their physical forms and left their beautiful cities behind to collapse and decay over the aeons, all remnants of the cities now crumbled to dust. Some people have experienced them as angels. They continued to inhabit the Earth and they also mastered the ability to travel from star to star. He gets a glimpse of how they do this, but it is too much for him to process, it flows through him and, he feels, out the other side without him being able to grasp it. They sometimes come together in containers such as the one in this room to correlate their experiences with one another in a more focused manner. And now he feels another type of energy flowing out from the box to him.

Now still with his eyes closed he sees a torrent of symbols such as the ones on the box streaming past him in a flood of information. The symbols are bright crimson against a black background, scimitars and curlicues and flowing lines and swirling spiral shapes going by so fast he can barely make them out. On and on it goes, a massive download of information flying past his inner eye. From left to right it flows, taking over his being and intercepting his mind. Now, just as quickly, it shifts directions and changes color, the symbols still the same kind and shape, but golden now and bronze, brightly gleaming against the field of black and flowing now from top to bottom, from high above to the depths of his soul. Streaming, streaming, flowing past and through him so fast he can barely make them out. These symbols seem absolutely alien and foreign to him yet also so familiar, an ancient language that must have served as the basis of every language that ever has been. It seems to be a combination of numerical forms and notes that could be translated into music—all these combining to form a symbolic record of thought. The symbols represent numbers which represent tones which represent colors which represent syllables which represent, at their most basic level, ideas—thought forms, which are essentially holographic transfigurations of energetic wave forms. These are being downloaded into him, transmitted in the form his mind's eye can most readily accept. And now even as his mind is being filled with this endless streaming download of information—though he knows not what it contains—a thought about the symbols enters his head. They are from this ancient civilization and these spirits who have lived upon Earth since that time millions upon millions of years ago, and they are also from Sirius— a planet from the star system Sirius. This is just a thought that comes to him, he doesn't know why he is getting this. Did these beings come to Earth from Sirius?

In the inner vision in his head the symbols flowing past appear to be slowing. And in the top right corner of the field of his inner vision he sees now an image of a face, a large head, with a bluish tint to it, as if it is looking down on him and then—it nods once and smiles. He can see it smiling at him, for just a brief instant, and then it is gone. Was it smiling at him in confirmation of this thought that the beings originally came from Sirius? Or was it simply smiling at him in recognition that he has successfully received whatever complex download of information has been transmitted to him... through him? He cannot be sure—there is no way of knowing. But the being smiling at him he takes to be a visual representation for his benefit, in the form he might recognize, of one of the spirits from within the box, a beneficent spirit, who has come here to help. He wants to let the family know that the box is okay, it will not harm them. Still, they will probably want to be rid of it, resting as it is in the center of their living room, blocking the view of the TV. He wants to open his eyes and say these things, but in the very selfsame instant that these thoughts are battling for room in his head, another vista opens before him and he can see a windswept hillside high above an open plain spreading with green fields far and wide below him. On the top of this steep hill is a formation of giant stones—slabs of granite ten feet tall arranged in a semi-circle facing out from the hilltop, towards the west, where the sun sets in the bosom of the valley below. Here now he turns to let the wind brush his face and he feels another presence with him, stuffed alongside him within the circle of stones, closer than the future and the extinguished moment just past, here now the presence of a commanding spirit different than the one who just nodded and smiled, totally different than the ones who were gathered in that box. He closes his eyes and sees them, yes, there is more than one. He has learned by now that he must close his eyes to truly see. A light shining at the lowest edge of his inner vision, pure blue silver white, and now another one off to the upper left,

this one more gleaming red and gold. These beings—
spirits—are not the same as the ones in the box, he
remembers them now as the same ones who were with
him in that beach house on that other planet where he
could put his hand through the book and through the
table. These are the same ones come to visit him again—
for some reason he thinks of them as the Council, though
he doubts they call themselves that. Now another one
appears far off to the right of his inner vision, golden
yellow in color, each of them with their distinctive
bandwidth, vibrating frequencies, they appear and
disappear, reappearing again in different places within the
glowing magenta darkness of his inner vision, his eyes still
closed to feel the wind on the top of that steep hill
howling past his face. He feels them intertwine with him,
approach and emerge, dilate and inflate within his
consciousness as long as cut down when one comes the
others come beneath the tempts and times already
launched and milking already how long the stars grow
feeling them intertwine within him coming to the front
door of his soul verified and scuttering keen with wisdom
lost not found keen with anything to say that he mayhaps
already knew three spirits gleaming in his vision
windswept on the pinnacle these have always been here
with him and guardians more than these hearing his
feeling, feeling his thoughts they speak to him they always
have been during his voyage saying to him speaking
directly to withstand him, saying 'As those beings used
that box for a moment to appear to you and to that family,

you use bodies to have presence in different timespace instants, reference points, you materialize your thoughts into physical expressions. The bodies you use are merely containers for these statements—these states—of your being. And these containers are in turn bundled up and stored within your soul—the bodies rest within the soul, not the other way round, and the soul in turn is merely the vessel that carries all of these things—stores them so to speak so that you may re-visit them when you need to, whenever you want to experience another facet of your being once again. All exist at once. There is no such thing as time. Thought creates time and time creates fear, as you have seen and felt. Time is merely a sequence of thought, and the feeling of sequence creates the sensation of lack, of fleeting things that one moment are here and the next are gone. You are not the body and you are not the mind, not the thoughts you think. You are not even the soul. The body is the container of the mind—of the thoughts you identify as you—and the soul is the container of these things, and even the soul is simply the vessel for all these facets of you.'

Eyes closed he feels them speaking, sees them hearing him think. The thought he thinks which they feel him hear is: 'If I'm not even the soul, then what am I?'

He knows they are aware of what he has thought to them, not spoken, and yet they think through him no more. He sees one of them glimmer silver white in a corner of his inner sight shining, pause there for an instant and disappear.

Wind brings him back to this place, opens his eyes again and stings them. His eyes water and he goes over to stand behind one of the giant stone slabs, feels it resonate with the force of the wind.

He places his palms against the stone and tries to hold in place the words, the thoughts they gave him. *The soul is just a vessel. I am not even the soul.*

And this thought he feels is like a launch pad, this thought and his palms pressed flat against the stone—they are a platform and a thought that sends him soaring up from the bald hilltop away from the wind and into the highest reaches where everything is possible; if he is not the body and not the mind and not even the soul, then what can he possibly be?

Another thought moment, another instant in timespace, another misdirection of his attention and he finds himself standing, once again, in the bedroom of their house in Entrevoir, on the cold stone floor at the top of the stairs—in the selfsame instant at the start of the party, back once more amongst the sounds of their little gathering of guests downstairs making forced small talk with their teen-aged son and daughter, wondering where the guest of honor himself might be, and, more likely, wondering when they will get to see the beautiful Marya make her appearance.

It will not be long—as he lets these sensations wash over him once more, just as strange to him now as the times and places he has been, as foreign to him as the lagoon in the pyramid city, as otherworldly as the spirit wind on Saturn or the spirits in that box in the 1950s living room, the echoing party noise that bounces up the stone stairway is as alien as the words those spirit beings thought through his head at the top of that windblown summit where the stone slabs have stood as guardian sentinels for ages upon ages. It will not be long, because as all of these visions pour themselves through him in utter contradiction of the moment he once again finds himself in, he watches with detached disinterest as Marya gracefully places the tip of her black high-heeled shoe on the next lower step of the stone stairway on her way down to the party, away from him, back turned to him, moving further and further away.

Lovely Marya—he has always wanted to lift her up. That was what the paintings were supposed to do. He would get a glimpse of the late afternoon light striking an abandoned automobile in a parking lot and he would seek in essence to take a snapshot of that instant in his head and then encapsulate every wavering fraction of shadow and intensity and pale remote reflection from that transient glimpse within the framework of the canvas over a period of days and weeks—sometimes months. In a way, now that he thinks about it, he was actually transmuting time, drawing that one moment out into days and weeks and months, lengthening it and stretching it out until it ended up being held in place as a permanent record, an eternal everlasting moment, bottled up and captured and transcribed onto the canvas. Projecting what had been in his mind at that moment into eternity. This process was—

is—he sees now, a way of raising up a single precise fleeting instant into a higher dimension—lifting it up and out of the stream of thought-invoked timespace into the higher realm wherein everlasting states of being reside. Translating a momentary thought or sense impression from a residual glimpse of the passing stream into its true and higher state, which is the Ideal form, the multi-faceted singularity of the eternal beingness of the highest Ideal of that object, person, place or thing—whatever it may be. This is how he has sought to capture beauty, because this he has always known: that he does not produce beauty in his paintings or his installation pieces, he captures it as true essence. That is what the installations are supposed to do as well—raise up and exalt. Lift up the person who is viewing them to a higher dimensional state of being—raise them up out of themselves, if only for a moment. That is what he has attempted to achieve with the piece called *Entrevoir,* waiting there at the top of the mountain for someone, anyone, to come and witness it. Maybe one of these people getting sloshed on campuget rosé will venture there, maybe Marya. She will have to see it at some point, since he dragged them all here for a year in order to create it. Will she still hate it on principle, even after she has allowed herself to experience it?

He has never really had a failure before. Perhaps it will be good for him, his legacy, to have a grand failure on his list of works. He can imagine the critics and art school profs deconstructing it already. "And don't forget, when Jacob Marsteller went to France to do *Entrevoir,* it still exists, though hardly anyone goes to see it. It is the one installation he never tore down—what an irony. His biggest failure is the only piece he ever allowed to remain in place."

Marya will love it one day—won't she? She will have to, she will look back fondly on these days with nostalgia, as he often does, even for times he experienced as a trauma or turmoil. When he looks back on those times years later he can see with some perspective that they may have been the best times, those days he struggled through filled even so with memories he wished he had savored even as they were happening. Marya will look back on this old stone house with fondness, even for this house she now hates, in this village she derides, this house they will be leaving soon, and she will remember the times when the kids were still young and the winter nights they spent at the kitchen table conjugating French verbs and trying to remember whether the word "cuillère" was masculine or feminine— how do they determine what gender a spoon is? And she will return here with him to visit again some day and he will walk with her up the winding labyrinth at the top of the mountain and she will see the vast sheets of gossamer metallic fabric shimmering in the sun and the wind and she will see, some day, the beauty in it.

Maybe not today, though. Not today, as she takes one more step, careful, careful not to turn her ankle in the high heels on the uneven stone at the landing, one more step away from him, her lovely hair at the back of her head receding from him in firm rebuke. The staircase seems to be telescoping his vision of her into a resounding idealized form that is locked in place, the roundness of her hips shadowed by the loose hang of her dress—black dress, of course—and the scalloped V of skin exposed at the back and shoulders, nothing but an outline of her, receding from him, lower and smaller as she places the sharp, tenuous point of her heel carefully on the next stone step away from him.

He cannot raise her up if she does not want to be. He cannot raise anyone up unless they want to be raised up. As an artist, he has learned that he cannot control the outcome. He can't control how many people come to look at his work, or what reactions they will have to it. Many billions upon billions of people will never come to see it. Many of those who do come to see it will not like it. But there will be a few whom he reaches, who have their gaze raised up for a moment or two, and in doing so he will have transformed them. He cannot control the outcome, but he can set forth his work for those who may be ready to be raised up and exalted.

There comes to him another sensation in the midst of the clamor from the room below—a series of tones, four distinctive notes he can hear in his head, not music from the party, this is music from a dream. Eyes closed again, another blink of an eye, and he is gone, transported from Entrevoir to a very large open interior space, dimly lit. Walking across the room, he feels the sensation of warmth, of being sheltered from the cold murky light of a late winter afternoon in the city—yes, it is New York,

Manhattan, but some time ago, many years ago, he can't be sure when. The room has other people in it and books, stacks of books. He goes to an old baby grand piano, which is not in great shape, it has seen a lot of use, the keys yellowed and uneven, the name of the maker nearly worn away above middle C: FEURICH. Still standing, he reaches down to the keys and begins to play, though he has never in his life as Jacob played any musical instrument. The chords that come forth are the ones he had just heard—four sonorous, elegiac chords struck in a slow, drawn out cadence. Then the pattern repeats with a slight variation, lifting *up* on the final chord instead of down—this is the key to the theme, the first sequence of chords descending, followed by the counterpoint of the same sequence resolving with an ascending major. He continues playing as if he has always known how to play, the notes flowing from his fingers with consummate skill. And as he plays, a man walks over to him and speaks:

"It is fine for you to play," the man says, "just play quietly."

The man must be the librarian. There are other people nearby, seated at long benches and tables, reading. They don't seem to mind his playing, perhaps they may even be enjoying it, so he does continue. The piece evolves from the initial theme he set forth, elaborating on the four-chord structure by adding an underlying slurred arpeggio for the left hand, developing along with the melody in a dream-like distant echo, as if a church choir were chanting along with him, almost as if it were a minuet. The melodic

115

four-chord structure he is playing with the right hand seems to be stuck in time, a solid edifice, whereas the underlying left-hand arpeggios seem to be trying to move the theme along from the past into the present.

The librarian comes over to him again, stands and listens to him playing for a moment. Then he once again speaks.

"You know, we have the original manuscripts for this here."

The librarian hands over a sheaf of musical score and he stops playing to take it.

The manuscript is old, yellowed, cracked at the corners, about to crumble if he grasps it too tensely. He recognizes in the quavers and demi-quavers of the first bars the theme he has been playing; this is his own piece, music he has composed. He sees the signature at the top of the page and recognizes it as his own.

And even though he had never played a single note of music in that other life as Jacob, here he can see the theme unfolding across the manuscript, can see within the chaotic dots and stems and prickling sharps and flats his own hand sprinkled across the page, the unfurling of a single idea into something superhuman, a thought form that emerges from a single stillpoint of meaning into a multi-dimensional object—it exists all at once as a single unitary being, something he can hold in his hands here, and also as a sequential flow like a stream that never stops moving water through it. He thinks of this as the progression of dimensions from a point to a line to a square to a cube—and then, what is beyond a cube? A hypercube, a cube cubed. A cube with a cube extending away from each face of it orthogonally. The music he just played on the piano is the hyper cube version of the two-dimensional notes his hand once wrote on this sheaf of manuscript paper many years ago. And now he knows within him what he meant by the theme—he remembers what he intended to convey with the two sets of four chords and the following two bars of four chords that resolve the theme, folding it back upon itself, as it were. Those four-chord sets were meant to represent death itself, that static ominous state we all came forth from and must all return to, that immense silent NO expressed in the form of those still and hanging chords even yet reverberating across the open space of the library reading room.

He nods to the librarian by way of thanks. Feels gratified to know that this man has recognized his work and that the manuscripts he created have a home here, they are valued. Suddenly, without having walked there, he finds himself outside on the sidewalk in front of the library, the street burdened by too many horses and motorcars trying to pass, a hum of noise electrifying the cold air even as the last shallow shred of daylight leaches from the sky between the buildings. He cannot be sure what year it is, but he knows he is visiting the city for a performance of one of his own works, he travels from city to city performing them, is famous for his performances of his works even as much as for the works themselves.

People hurry past him—they are nearly all shorter than him, and he seems to look down on their heads from a great height as they pass. He has a cap on and a heavy beige camelhair coat that comes down to his knees. They do not recognize him for who he is, the famous composer and concert pianist, visiting their city for a few days, standing in their midst, but that's okay. He knows who he is, knows that he has been sent here to lift them up. His music does this, he has seen it, felt it, when the performance goes well, feels the people in the audience elevated to a higher place when the applause rings out and lifts, lifts—the applause is for him but it is also for the way the performance has made the people feel, the appreciation they emit is for having been raised from the realm of the cube to the realm of the hypercube, the space where time does not exist, where the ideal form of an idea, a concept such as *death* does exist in all its rich and variegated meanings. Where he can lead the audience around it and help them experience this ideal form from every angle and expression and feeling. For on this super-dimensional plane analytical thought no longer holds true; the meanings can only be expressed and determined through feeling, the knowledge that exists within the heart. That is what he has tried to convey through his compositions, through his performances.

He watches the mass of people flow past him and knows that he must head now towards the concert hall to prepare for this evening's performance. It is getting late. He must allow himself plenty of time to warm up, to let the fingers loosen from the grip of the cold. Yes, *death*. That is what he had been trying to capture in the theme of that piece he had been playing. A transition which is also an everlasting steady state. How to place that into the form of music? Surely, though, music is the best way to capture it, to express it, for, as he understood when he held his own hand-written score in his hands a few moments ago, that chord progression he wrote exists forever as a static entity, and yet it can also unfold at any moment as a transformation through the playing of the sequence of tones. And through the performance and hearing of these tones, the feeling of death, which is its only true and certain understanding, can be accomplished.

As he begins walking, he looks around once more at the people passing him on the sidewalk, dozens of people walking past. Each of them will die, this is a certainty. Only the when and where are unknown. Seeing them pass by him this way, as beings who are destined to perish, he knows that he is here to lift them up, that is his chosen pursuit, the purpose of his music, his art. The thought that each face he sees, each man, woman and child he passes, will die makes him cherish each of them, makes him understand that each of these beings, though there are millions of them even in this single city, is worth being cherished. If he could, he would embrace every single one of them as they passed, would raise them up from this world where only one destination awaits them.

Why, he wonders, why have his thoughts turned to this? He keeps walking towards the concert hall, watching the eyes of all those who pass, though their eyes turn away. He would save each of them, if he could, and the thought of saving them blacks out his vision and makes his head grow cold. He is no longer walking, no longer that great composer, neither invested in the world nor prepared to relinquish it so soon. He has realized the primary error of our existence but hasn't yet established it in his own existence. This is what's taking him to another fixed-motion holograph of experience. This is what transports him down that never-ending corridor towards an open field outside the walls of another great city at some much earlier date, a new place where he has already been.

He stands now, clothed in a loose robe of finest satin, at the head of a giant mass of men, an army that has besieged this city for many weeks, and has finally, he knows, on this day broken through the walls and triumphed. That is the feeling he gets, flowing through him as he stands there on the grassy plain looking at the battered walls before him. He has triumphed, his will has prevailed, as it always must. A call of trumpets sounds from the ranks of horsemen behind him, announcing his next command. Yes, he must command what will happen next, as always. This sudden sensation of being thrown into this man's head has caused him to pause for a moment, and the man to his right—his lieutenant—looks to him with expectation.

As he stands there, deciding, remembering, what he wants to happen next, a vision of all that has led up to this moment floods his senses, a torrent of all the days and weeks that have gone by overwhelms him, allowing him to live all those many moments in a single instant.

They had surprised the city-dwellers by locating a distant ford of the Syr Darya River, far to the north, and riding over four hundred miles across the Kyzyl Kum desert. None of the city-dwellers nor their leaders had expected that an army could traverse this vast and barren wasteland, but they did not know him nor his horses nor his men. He and his men are accustomed to life in the wastes of the Great Desert and the immense open expanse of the steppes along the Onon River, surviving for weeks on dried meat, dried curd, and milk paste. This ride had been harsh, but nothing he and his men had not done before. When he and his many men had arrived at the walls of the great city, an advance force of Turkish mercenaries from the city had attempted to repel us before we could lay siege. In fact, the Turks had not even given us credit for being able to construct the engines necessary to blockade a city—one of the captured Turks had admitted as much under torture. The Turks did not realize that our yaks and camels carried the dismantled pieces of all the mechanisms necessary to breach the city's walls, assembled by the cordon of Chinese engineers who travel with us.

The Turks and the Shah's Viceroy of the city had thought that we were a disorganized horde of vandal horsemen, easy to rout, and we did all we could to allow them to think this. When they first approached us, we sent a small band of light cavalry to charge at them in a most disorganized manner, screaming wildly, horses galloping headlong and out of rank, some of them pretending to retreat. This encouraged the Turks to move all their forces forward together as one into our trap. Once they charged and our light cavalry had absorbed with skill and bravery all they could endure, we sounded the chilling beat of the naccara and the ranks of the heavy cavalry moved forward at a steady trot, bearing down on the suddenly confused and frightened Turks in silence, all the while our Chinese engineers caused the catapults to hurl explosives into their midst, and our riders hidden at the flanks encircled them and rained arrows upon them and prevented any chance of retreat. The Turks were doomed. A small band of them had decided to desert their own comrades and join our side, appealing to us that they would help show us the way to enter the city by breaching the walls at their weakest point. We allowed them to join us, but only for the evening, while we fed them, gave them mare's milk and koumiss to drink, tended to their wounds, and listened to what they had to tell us about the city we were about to conquer. These Turks were traitors, and congratulated themselves for having the foresight to join our force. There is nothing he and his men deplore more than a traitor, and so once we learned all we could gather, he had Qaciün lead them to some tents to rest for the evening and there Qaciün and his men slaughtered them by slitting their throats. There is nothing more despicable than a traitor.

We allowed some of the Turkish advance force to escape and return to the city, to let the Viceroy and his garrison know we had arrived, and to spread fear and terror amongst the citizens there. We allowed their lives to be spared for the purpose of spreading fear and terror, for often this will encourage a city to simply surrender without a fight. There is no purpose in fighting and losing good horses and men and potentially destroying a city containing valuable plunder. Better to leave the city intact and bring the wealth back to Karakorum. Yet in this case the Viceroy was a proud man and determined to fight. We received no signal of surrender once our force surrounded the city walls.

The siege spanned the period of five months. Our Chinese engineers and the strong slaves we brought assembled the catapults and mangonels and battered the walls from every direction. Several of the watchtowers fell. We allowed no food to enter the city and their foodstuffs ran short. We received word from our spies that the inhabitants were starving. We requested the Viceroy to offer his surrender, providing him one final chance to spare his citizens our wrath, advising him that if he surrendered now the city would remain intact, we would not burn it to the ground. He ignored our offer, and so we turned our full attention to the weakest point in the walls, of which the traitorous Turks had told us. There, at the northeast corner, after sustained battering from the mangonel, we noticed that the foundations of the wall were supported by wooden piers. This had been a swamp at one time, the point of the city closest to the river, perhaps at one time the port, before the fortifications were built. The piers were meant to shore up the foundations on the marshy ground, and we set them on fire using buckets of pitch. The foundations crumbled and the walls sagged and buckled under the pounding of our twenty pound stones. Once this was accomplished, it was an easy task for our light cavalry to charge and breach the walls.

We avoided much hand to hand fighting, for once the Viceroy saw that the walls were broken, he sent word to us that he wished to surrender, hoping to spare his own skin. But this was too late—he had not accepted our final and most generous offer. We entered the city and I commanded the men not to plunder in a disorganized fashion, for this leads to waste. Nevertheless, certain of the men fell upon the women of the town and raped them, slaughtering many of the women and their kin. This was against the order and these men were duly chastised and punished by having a portion of their plunder dispersed to others. The city was indeed beautiful to behold. As we walked its lanes and wide avenues, the shopkeepers cowered behind their shuttered storehouses. The Viceroy cowered in the citadel with his garrison, but he could be dealt with in due course. The most impressive stone building lay at the foot of the mount which bore the citadel. We entered this building and asked what its purpose was. A man dressed in purple robes, their chief shaman it would appear, told us it was the house of worship to their god, called Allah. We had never beheld a building of such beauty. Clearly, there was much of value in this city and the Shah's empire. Clearly, we had chosen a worthy destination for our campaign.

Our men and horses needed meat and fodder. Mounting the altar, the order was given by me to their shaman to open the shops and storehouses of the city so that our men could eat and our horses be fed. The shaman nodded even as he was praying to his god Allah, sometimes whispering, sometimes aloud. We brought the horses into their temple and fodder was brought for their forage. We built fires on the stone floors of the temple, and our men cooked meat the storekeepers brought for a feast. After we ate and filled our bellies for the first time in months, the command was given by me to begin pillaging.

Though some of the men had disobeyed me and raped a portion of the women, most of the city and its wares remained in tact. We informed the shaman that if he and the shopkeepers allowed us to enter without a fight, the city would be spared. He agreed to this, and so we began the plunder.

Every man had earned the right to carry off what he could, and this was done. We herded the inhabitants of the city outside the walls. Entering the shops and storehouses, we found jewels of all colors and sizes, fine carpets, leather-bound books and parchments, spices, rag paper, glassware, chain mail and armor and scimitars we could use in further campaigns. Though the shaman broke down in tears as we removed these items from the city, we could hear the shaman also praying, praying aloud to his god continuously.

This was all done and the remembrance of these things flashed through his head as if in a single moment. Now the command for what is to be next must be given. He must command what will happen next, as always.

Several things, all at once.

He commands the Chinese clerks to herd the frightened inhabitants into various groups, separating those with special abilities or talents to the far left of the field—those who can speak several languages are useful, those who are skilled artisans, those who are poets, architects, artisans or scientists, musicians or physicians, those are useful and should all be spared. He commands the Chinese clerks to herd all those strong young men to the center of the field, for those will be useful as slaves to build earthworks and siege engines and carry loads in the campaigns to come, some of them useful to be sold as slaves in faraway markets; he commands the Chinese clerks to herd all those strong young women into another portion of the field, separate from their men, for those are useful also.

He commands the Chinese clerks to herd the remaining inhabitants into the far right of the field, the halt and the lame, the old ones, the youngest children, for those will need to be dealt with in a different manner.

And he commands the light cavalry, the fastest and bravest of his force, to storm now the citadel and bring back the Viceroy alive.

As the light cavalry begin their charge back into the barren city, we begin to do what must be done. As the heavy cavalry stand watch over the artisans and young men from the city, our officers look upon the strong young women who are available to us. For the first time in months we have women in our midst.

He goes amongst them and chooses the one whom he desires to have. The other officers do the same. She is a dark-haired one, with high cheek-bones such as he likes, and eyes darker than the night. Her skin however shines with a pale whiteness unlike the women of Karakorum, and this makes him desire her all the more. He places his knife upon the white skin of her throat and stares into her obsidian eyes. She returns his gaze with a look of sheer terror. He grasps her robe and pulls it over her head, then shoves her to the ground. As he does this, the others begin to do the same. Women scream and moan. Their men who must watch this begin to weep. Fear is the chief mechanism of conquering—he must inject fear into this woman. He grabs her behind the knees and pushes her legs into the air, so that he may enter her. He lifts his own satin robes and shoves himself inside, feeling for the first time in months the silky sheath of a woman's body. He slaps her face and bites her shoulder as he thrusts—he is not loving her as he loves his wife. He is conquering her. He is shoving himself as far into her as he can, entering the womb of her kingdom even as he is entering the Shah's. Shoving her harder and harder and smacking her once again until he can hear her scream. When she is screaming loud enough he can release—it does not take long, after all these months. The screaming of the other women and their men helps him release. And then it is finished.

He could have another, if he wants, or this one again, but he must turn his attention to the rest of the plunder, must dispose of this city and there is still the Viceroy to dispose of, disturbing his thoughts.

He stands and kicks the woman as she lies there, sobbing. Kicks her in the ribs. She will make a fine slave for someone in Karakorum.

Some of the cavalrymen have joined the officers and princes in raping the women. They will disgrace them until the men have all been satisfied, many will take them more than once in many ways. Screaming and moaning from the women and shouts of supplication from their men standing by helplessly watching. A messenger arrives from the light cavalry—there is hand to hand fighting with the Viceroy and his guard at the citadel. There have been many casualties to our men. The messenger looks to him for a decision, a command. He turns and looks at the vast plain around him, surveys it for a sign of what to do. He does not want to destroy the city—better to save it and have it produce wares for the good of the people of Karakorum. What sign shall be given, what command?

A horseman is raping a woman on the ground a few feet away from him, shoving himself into her while she lies there and sobs. The noise from the screaming women is beginning to annoy him. The one he raped himself lies there on the ground at his feet and stares at him with a look of fear and hatred—fear, this is what he must remember. Fear conquers all and must be spread to other parts of the Shah's kingdom. No more casualties, enough of all this.

The woman he has taken lies at his feet watching, not understanding what is going on. She would make a good slave at his tent in Karakorum—he could take her along with him throughout the rest of the campaign and penetrate her whenever he pleases. This would be a welcome companionship. Perhaps in due course she would bear him children. He looks to her for a sign, reaches his hand toward her. Her eyes are filled with hatred for him. He reaches his hand down to help her to her feet. Instead of taking his hand, she spits at it, gobs of white spittle landing on his palm and wrist.

He withdraws his hand and stares at her, having received his sign.

He nods to the messenger and gives his command: "Burn the city to the ground. Not one stone of this city shall be left standing. When the wooden buildings have burned, make these strong men and women tear down the buildings of stone with their bare hands and pile all the rubble in the moat. Not one stone of their city shall remain standing—I want to see it as a smouldering ruin." He spits at the woman on the ground beneath him, a stream of spit covering her hair and forehead, her black eyelashes. The messenger nods and turns on his mount to ride back into the city that will soon be burnt to the ground.

"Now the time has come to kill all the children and the old ones, the halt and the lame." He pulls his blade from its scabbard and spits once more in the face of that woman who dared to disgrace him, aiming his spit towards her dark and hateful eyes. The cavalrymen set upon the old men and women, slashing their throats, gutting the small children as well. The men of the city stand by helplessly watching and the women scream louder now as they watch their children succumb to the slaughter, high-pitched wails of terror and despair. This one at his feet would have made a beautiful slave but she should not have disgraced him in front of all who watch. He presses the blade to her belly which could have borne him children and waits, to make sure all his men and all the men of the city can see this. There will be none to disobey him—they will see now that his sword will spare no one. He remembers himself plunging himself inside her and leans the blade into her belly, slicing it open like the belly of a calf the skin opens easily and the blade slips in as far as he can push it, until it touches bone. Her obsidian eyes open wider and stare at him in disbelief, as if she somehow thought he would want to have her after what she did to him. No. She will suffer and perish. He lifts the blade up a bit and thrusts it towards the ribs, tearing through her gut. No more children will come from here, no more bearing of enemy warriors. She lets out a muffled groan, blood gurgling in her throat, the blade slashing through her sternum and ribs, her breasts torn apart. Beautiful breasts for suckling, will never suckle any more.

"Kill them, all the women and children, kill them all," he shouts. "Bring only the strong men as slaves—all the rest shall perish."

There must be fifteen hundred to slaughter, the killing will take several hours. The heads of the shaman and his priests will be stacked in a pyramid above the moat where the bodies and the rubble of the city will be dumped. He wants to see this city leveled, nothing left but a smoking ruin. He looks once more at the dying woman at his feet and stomps his boot on her stomach, entrails spilling from her wound. And her eyes widen, obsidian pools of fear, open as wide as the night of the new moon, shocked by the final sensations they will ever endure. Those black eyes engulf him in their darkness open so wide the darkness he has engendered here on this plain and in other cities, other lives is so broad and deep it engulfs him in its enormity vast as the black vacuum of space between one galaxy and the next. The blackness of space surrounds him and draws him away from here, lifts him up into the violet majesty of the highest atmosphere where the air is so thin he can no longer breathe. He feels himself being lifted away from the slaughter and feels a strange calmness overtake him, all the fear and destruction left behind. He is being raised up slowly, ever higher, sailing above the earth so high he can see the curvature of the broad horizon, a blue arc tinged with pale wisps of cloud in the distance. Lifted up, he can see the folds of mountains tucked one upon the other like a blanket that has been wadded up by a child who has awoken from a restless night of sleep, and beyond them, in the distance, the curved arc of the earth is swathed with a huge lake, stretching to the far horizon, its two shores converging towards a point they never reach. This is larger than any lake—it must be the Caspian Sea, flanked on the right by a broad pale desert devoid of any markings. His awareness wheels about, turns to see what is on the opposite horizon, even as he is being lifted ever higher, soaring miles above the earth. Another range of mountains, folded one upon the other, as if the earth had been squeezed in a giant vise. Beyond these mountains, another sea, an oblong of blue water glistening with a slab of desert stretching out beyond it. His mind's eye can see it laid out before him and he recognizes it, as if he has been raised up to look at a map of the planet—this is the Persian Gulf with the vast desert of the Arabian peninsula beyond. And as he wheels around further, lifting ever higher, he sees the dark enormity of the true ocean waters to the south, the true ocean engulfing the full horizon now he sees that most of the earth is water, vastness of the ocean spreading far beyond the crumpled mass of land beneath him. Ever higher he goes and he understands that he is being raised beyond the earth so that his sins may be left behind, he knows that the vastness of the waters spread before him is the Indian Ocean and he is seeing the full shoreline of southwest Asia so high is he now above the planet. Though his sins be as scarlet, they shall be washed whiter than snow. This is the thought that reaches him from that deadly scene so far below him. All is revealed and reveiled, all shall be transmitted and transmuted by the enormity of the vastness of creation. None shall perish, none shall be lost. No man is slave to another, only to his own transgressions, his own fears and misgivings. When he has been raised up high enough that he ceases to see, his consciousness, awareness, is drawn again within, to a still point of nothingness and derision.

Somehow he must be saved. His awareness floats in a black still nothingness beyond decisions beyond all the choices he made beyond love and greed beyond all traces of sin. In blackness his awareness is washed away his reward is God's alone to consider and dispense. His eyes are no longer tarnished by the view of the slaughter he left behind, his conscious awareness is drawn together to a still point of being surrounded by the empty vastness of blank and open space wherefore then do ye harden your hearts whence does he happen upon the next happenstance of his advancement of knowing? In a dim instant moment of traveling from the shores of one galaxy to the next he traverses the breadth of the universe for time does not exist nor distance in the stillpoint of pure awareness only being has become one point one moment one instantaneous here and now. However ungodly are his deeds, his godliness is only apparent here in this instant his awareness opens itself upon the horizon of the firstborn objects of the galaxies of the stars the universe spawned. His pernicious derision no longer prescient no longer converted nor concealed half an hour of morning's glory bitter water of karmic deeds distilled and disdained neither bundled up nor clothed upon the framework of his soul. All here now is laid bare. His conscious awareness opens to see a cosmic object laid out before him, whiteness shining forth in the midst of the open black vacuum of space though he is in the gap between the vast distances of stars and it should be black as deepest midnight he left behind the object shining forth before him has made the void sparkle with searing milky white light.

Radiance surrounds him, radiance and joy. The searing white globe of this object which is larger than any star could be is laid out before him and it is impossible to judge its vastness, there is nothing to gauge it, to measure it against. It could be as far across as his own solar system, the star and planets from whence he came, yet it is one object, spinning spinning so rapidly now he sees because from the back side of it there comes something terrifying in its magnificence, a column of fire as broad as a thousand suns all antiquities rendered irrevocable rendered lord of the sheep the shepherd sweeps around for the moving sumptuous nearness of the fire sweeping towards him the shepherd of the burning fire light fixt in its glory bound and frightening in its heaven-sent outlandish quasar heavens were opened and respected in their phantasm restored to the light of a thousand suns beaming in a column of hot white light even searing brighter than the globe of light from whence it emits.

This he sees now and understands this radiance is a jet of pure transmission this radiance from this globe of pure white light is a pulsing intelligence that is a living being of its own radiating the light of pure thought across the galaxies which in time in due course over thirty billions of years will someday reach his own though he now is here with it in this very selfsame moment space and time, this column of brilliance if it reaches him will engulf him and consume him in its bluish bright white light this pulsating object is ALIVE.

His next thought is to abandon this place and all its glory is too much for him, too much. This object is one of the first beings in the universe, one of the first-born of God, the ancient of ancients, shedding the light of pure thought upon the far reaches of distant space from whence he came. He can feel it has been waiting for him to witness, waiting to purge and illuminate his soul. The column of white fire swings around the horizon and grows to fill his point of view, if it reaches him he will be immersed in it he will no longer exist. Radiance intelligence pulsing first-born of God shimmering overcoming possession of doubts confession of the time which is nigh sinners sin with proficiency with hallowed authority and increase all sins are washed into pure whiteness hast thou seen this O son of man, hast thou borne witness to the whiteness which shall come to pass? First-born beloved sun of God here shimmering shining joy and pure radiance down through the ages upon ages willst thou stand forth and bear this crown upon thine head?

No, he must not see it must not let it wash over him, for if it does he will be washed away forever. There must be another way for him to wash away his sins.

His awareness flicks from this place to another closes down shuts itself away he is learning now to control it, turning his awareness away from one thing towards another makes that bright column of light that quasar melt away and only blackness here remains. Has he learned enough to fulfill his own intentions with awareness has he learned to send his awareness where he may want it to go? With only blackness before him he cannot think of what may come next, his only thought had been to escape the certain annihilation of his Self by that towering column of light. He had felt its presence its beingness its own conscious awareness dwarfing his own—the presence of its raw enormous intelligence had frightened him more than anything he had ever felt or known so where now will the blankness of his thinking feeling take him?

The blackness around him now feels less like the vacuum between stars and more like the void within his own awareness. The gulf of blank space is no longer what he must traverse—the distances have been reduced to those within him, space turned inside out. Ever onward goes this black beyond, until he opens his eyes again and feels himself drawn into another aspect of his being, another way in which his existence serves to reconcile itself.

Here he is, in another body, another life of his own to be. He finds himself in the dusty dungarees of a man from the frontier era of the American west, thin-worn denim and a leather vest, no hat on his head, slouched in the saddle of a horse with the heavy knotted presence of a noose around his neck.

"Is that all of them?"

A man astride a horse with a loose shuffling drawl shouts across the dirt street to another man. Both of them holding shotguns.

"All we could round up for now. This one is the ringleader, been helping the savages tear down our fences."

The man must be talking about him, for he is pointing the barrel of his shotgun directly at him. As he looks about, he sees that there are three other men seated on horses with nooses around their necks, the same way he is, flanked on either side by the two men with the shotguns. He turns his head more and sees people from the town, some of whom he recognizes, who have gathered here in this street to watch him die. Behind him, beyond the townspeople, a pile of dead bodies is stacked in a heap in the middle of the muddy road. Maybe twenty or so, all freshly slaughtered, all natives of this land. Why is he about to be murdered? What has he to do with the pile of dead men, women, and children on the street behind him? It doesn't seem to be that he had anything to do with killing them—he is being killed along with them.

"Okay, on my signal," the first man says, "whip the horses and make 'em run."

The other man with a gun comes over astride his horse and places a black hood over the head of the man seated next to him. Then his turn is next, the damp scratchy cloth of the hood closing down his vision. The other two must be having hoods placed on them as well.

He can feel his own breath reflected back to him from the shroud of the hood against his face. In this moment it comes back to him, the life he has been living here—a writer for the newspaper of the town, he has been publishing articles denouncing the way the settlers have been taking the natives' land and converting it to farms and ranches, he has been helping the natives get rid of the fences the ranchers have used to cordon off the prairie for their cattle to graze. Denouncing the slaughter of natives when they won't leave. Now he is about to be slaughtered along with them.

No. He won't be hung this way, on his own horse. Better to die trying than be executed again. Though his hands are bound behind his back, he figures he can make himself fall if he throws himself forward over the horse's left shoulder—but wouldn't the noose still break his neck? Perhaps, but worth a try; the alternative is certain death. It's possible, he calculates, that if he launches himself off the horse he can do it with less force and a better angle than if the horse runs out from under him and then maybe he can slip this noose from his neck. Not much of a chance, but it's something.

In the instant before he makes his move, the air becomes still and he hears something totally out of synch with the horror he feels: the oblivious warbling melody of a robin, singing its joyful tune, calling out across the windless morning sky to let every being present know the wonders of the day to come.

He rears back to provide extra momentum, then heaves himself headfirst across the neck of the horse. It is a longer fall than he ever would have imagined. The hood over his head makes it feel like he is falling into that vast and open void once more. On his way to the ground, the noose tightens around his throat and latches on, snapping the vertebrae with a loud pop exceeded only by the explosion of the shotgun firing a few feet from his back. The force of the hot lead piercing his body twists him around the opposite direction as the horse rears up and crumples to the ground beneath him, shot through with the spray of errant slugs and his own blood. All the air the spirit of his being is released from him as his body swings in a spiraling arc around the pivot of the sharp break point where the noose has severed his spine all the spirit of his being continues to fly forward in its flight not constrained by the barriers of his bones or torso or limbs or corpus collosum he has launched himself out of his body and into a long long tunnel of dazzling rainbow light of every color fleeing forward into this tunnel he sees now which is dying which is death if he lets himself fly forward and finish his fall he will be all the way dead yet there is no more choosing here he is no longer at choice the colors flash past him in their forward fleeing flow slender and never mistaken intricate as the opposite white nightfall of the living day that robin will have that he will never see, the colors flow by and leach their brightness away until he is on to something new a sliver of white diminishing illumination his spirit is still falling forward will it never reach the ground? In the various bright whiteness of his being there is a moment of realization here a thought crosses his awareness in bright broken boldness flashing by: THOUGH MY SINS BE AS SCARLET THEY SHALL BE WASHED WHITER THAN SNOW. Whiter than snow is his being now, all the colors have been melted away somewhere some day that robin is still singing its joyful song and here he is attenuating his own awareness of his being to come forth again anew in another life expression to be born again anew for he has come to know that death and birth are merely transmutations of energy are one and the same thing.

His eyes open and he is in a second story room, staring out the window at the branches and leaves of a tree whose trunk he cannot see. Across the lawn and down the slope of a slight hill is the brick exterior of the main building, the building he has come to think of in this life as the central core. The granite keystone that sits atop the doorway announces the date to him, or at least a close approximation of where he must be in time: 1917. The central core is where they take him for his treatments, where they try to wash away all the visions of the lives that he can see. They try to tell him not to hear the voices of the lives he knows are here, they make him talk to the doctors but the doctors do not know what is happening all around him.

He sees visions, hears voices talking to him, talking through him, he says the words sometimes that he hears in his head aloud, and this confuses the doctors and nurses, this rambling speech of his is what first made his mother and father bring him to the doctors and ask them what was wrong. Just a moment ago, staring out the window at the leaves on the tree and the building across the lawn, he saw four men on horses with hoods on their heads, he heard a man say, "whip the horses and make 'em run."

He said it himself, several times, over and over again, as if he were trying out the sounds of the words in his mouth:

"Whip the horses and make 'em run. Whip the horses and make 'em run." Trying to get the sounds right, just the way that man said them. He begins to raise his voice now, saying it louder. "Whip the horses and MAKE 'em *run*." As he lets these words come out, it feels as if his vision is going dark, as if the light is going out of his head.

The nurse comes in to see what's going on. One of the nurses he likes—she's young and thin, bony elbows and a hooked nose that reminds him of a school teacher he used to have before they brought him here.

"What's the matter, Bennie. What is it?"

"Whip the HORSES and make 'em RUN." He sees the darkness around his head melt into a long tube of rainbow colors, violet and yellow, green and blue and gold sailing past him, tilts his head to make them go away. He feels the nurse put her arm around his shoulders.

"We're going to take you down to see Dr. Evans in a few minutes and then it will be time for lunch. You like to talk to Dr. Evans."

He doesn't answer her—she keeps her arm around his shoulders, across his back, trying to give him some comfort, though she has no idea what's happening to him or what he is talking about. He wishes she would go away and leave him alone, and at the same time wants to have her hold him tight, make the voices go away. Another voice, another vision invades his head now. Walking down the street in a huge city, with dozens of people walking past him. He has a cap on his head. It only lasts an instant and then another voice, a thought is in his head, words he hears in a ghostly echo and begins to repeat.

"Though my sins be as scarlet... though my sins be as scarlet."

"Bennie," the nurse comes around to look at him, look into his eyes. "What are you talking about? Can you tell me what you see?"

He sees stacks of dead bodies piled on a dirt road. He sees a man with a shotgun on a horse, staring at him. And those words in his head trying to get out. "Though my sins be as scarlet... sins be as scarlet."

"Come on Bennie, come with me. We're going to see Dr. Evans."

She slips her arm around his elbow and hoists him from the chair by the window. He doesn't resist. His body is almost limp, his legs don't want to raise him up, but he does stand and go with her. She doesn't know what's happening to him, but he likes her, likes to feel her arm around his, feel the warmth of her long bony body walking next to him.

"My neck hurts," he says, as they proceed down the long corridor lined with rooms where the other patients reside. "Neck feels like—wham!"

"Where does it hurt?"

Walking with her has made some of the voices go away. He can focus now on the cream-colored paint on the walls slipping by them, not a lot of colors here, only one. He points to the left side of his neck, touches it with three fingers at the left side, near the base. It feels as if he has been bludgeoned with a baseball bat here. That is always the problem, he has so many feelings and sensations happening at once, it's hard to focus on any single thing and keep it from slipping away. They all seem to come out of nowhere, bubbling up to the surface in competition with each other, as if all the stations on a radio receiver were tuned in at the same time. And then there are people like this nurse—he can't even remember her name—trying to ask him questions. It's as if every leaf on that tree, every pane of glass in the window of his room, were trying to convert themselves into sound and speak through him. All the channels of the radio on at once.

The doctors and nurses are kind to him, they just can't understand. He likes to talk with Dr. Evans, they are in his office now, Dr. Evans is the one who understands the most, tries hard to know what it must feel like to be inside his head. The office of Dr. Evans is a warm-feeling place, walls lined with books and a couch where it is nice to sit for a while and talk. Sometimes he can sit there for an hour or two and talk with Dr. Evans about things without having voices come through. Dr. Evans brings him a cup of hot tea to drink.

"Hello Bennie, how are you doing today?"

"Just fine—are you going to take me for treatment?"

Sometimes Dr. Evans and one of the nurses take him to central core for the treatments and that is not something he likes.

"Not today, Bennie. Today we're just going to sit here a while and talk, and maybe give you some medicine to take along with your tea."

"I need to see Joseph. When is Joseph coming to visit again?"

"Joseph won't be back for a while. But I know he will come to see you again soon."

"Joseph hasn't been here in a long time—why?"

"Joseph loves you, and your mother and father love you. They will be back again soon."

Dr. Evans writes something down in a notebook, smiles at him from behind his desk. The nurse is sitting with him, still close by on the couch. He tries to remember what they were talking about the last time he was here in Dr. Evans' office. It seems like it was a very long time ago, but it could have been only yesterday. They were talking about Joseph, his brother, he was asking them if they could tell him what Joseph was doing these days. He would like to be able to flip a switch somehow and shut out all of these voices, these visions in his head, and go back to live with his family once again. Dr. Evans and the nurses are trying to help him do this, he knows, and they are kind to him nearly every day, except for some of the treatments in central core—those treatments are not nice. He often tries to tell Dr. Evans everything he can remember about what it was like before the voices started coming through, when he lived at home with Joseph and his mother and father in their home in Rochester. It's a beautiful big white house with a lawn that goes on forever, where he and Joseph used to play baseball for hours and his father would arrive home from his work in his automobile sputtering up the long drive to the carriage house in back. That one day he can remember—the first day the voices started coming through, he thought it was Joseph talking to him or his father from the next room. But it was from nowhere in the house or out on the lawn, the voices come from inside his own head and he has never been able to figure out how to get them to stop. The voices have been evolving over time, they have changed over to something more now—he tries to tell the doctors and nurses—more like visions, as if he were being taken over by somebody else's life. Like the four men on the horses, with those terrible hoods over their heads; when those visions fill his mind they are more real than anything in the room around him.

"Joseph loves me."

"Yes, he loves you very much and misses you. He told me so himself."

He told me so… he told me so. He must try to hold on to these thoughts, his own thoughts, his own voice, so they will block out the other ones when they come into his head.

"Tell Joseph I love him."

"I will Bennie," Dr. Evans says, he even makes a note of it on his pad of paper. "Next time I see him I will tell him."

From somewhere near the ceiling of Dr. Evans' office, he hears the sound of a bird singing. Lovely warbling tune, four notes repeated in sequence, suddenly make him glance up to the corner of the ceiling to look for a bird that is not there. But the song is, the four calling notes of a bird signing it's lovely song. He looks around the room, the ceiling, to see if he can find it.

"What do you see Bennie?"

He sees the ceiling, the woodwork, the crown molding and hears the bird calling and hears another voice and he repeats what it is saying.

"This one is the ring-leader… this one is the ring-leader." The ceiling melts into liquid swirling down a drain as the voices force their way into his head and out through his own voice. He can see four men on horses, their heads cowled with black hoods. "On my signal… Whip the HORSES and make 'em RUN." Then other voices start forcing their way through, erupting out through him, other voices, other visions: "Come thou to me, Asar. O thou who art called aloud—Asar, come forth!" The floodgates are opened, Spirit is flooding through him, the voices and images are overwhelming, his mouth is repeating the words that burst through. "Tomas, haben wir für Sie kommen. Tiazque yehua xon ahuiacan. Annochipa tlalticpac... do you suppose that our Father would suffer His own son to be *enslaved*?"

From a dim corner of his awareness, he hears the doctor calling out to him, perhaps he is even shouting, but the doctor's voice is not even a whisper compared to what is happening in his own head. Images of a temple mount, high above an ancient city made of stone and straw huts. Image of a town square with a tall gothic cathedral, image of a woman touching his bare chest, then drawing away. Stars, blackness, emptiness of space. Cold broken stillness and despair. And the voices keep coming through him: "The soul is just a vessel I am not even the soul the veil of the temple is rent asunder O thou who art called aloud— open thine eyes and see do ye this in remembrance of me Ich bin in der Gnade nicht unter dem Gesetz though my sins be as scarlet they shall be washed whiter than snow."

The floodgates are opened, the overwhelming abundance of Spirit is flowing through. There are no boundaries between him and anyone else, anything else. Even with these voices coming through his mouth and his head, he can feel the presence of Dr. Evans with him, can feel the walls and the bookshelves around him even as if he is within them.

"Hexe, Hexe, ihn zu töten! It's haunted, there are ghosts in it. Now the time has come to kill all the children and the old ones, the halt and the lame."

Image of hundreds of men on horses, swords drawn, cutting men down, slicing them clean through. Sound of high wind soaring, crowding against his face. Droning sound of an engine, something his mind cannot understand, the image, the sensation of flying up amongst the clouds. Yes, he is flying now, seated in a small compartment, in some kind of contraption that is similar to his father's automobile, but he is driving it up in the sky! He feels his hands on either side of something similar to a steering wheel and then moves his right hand over to grasp the handle, a lever coming out of the floor of the contraption. The clouds are moving very fast, the sound of the wind whistling against the windows wrapped around his head within this tight narrow space. He pulls back on the lever but there is only the sensation of the floor dropping away from under him, the powder puff clouds and clear sky circling up and over his head and the shocking sight of cornfields and the hard broad earth wheeling into view. The cornfields are coming at him very fast now, as if some invisible force has begun pushing them towards him. They are growing so huge within his field of vision that he can make out the individual rows now and, off to one side, he can see a wire fence and a sea of prairie grass blowing in the wind. He will hit the earth head on very soon—it is growing so huge it fills the windscreen coming at him like a giant wall. He jerks back on the lever with his right hand one more time and hears the engine of this machine lift its ragged voice in anguish, failing in its mission to raise him once again above the ground.

Then, he notices something else, in the final seconds before the full disaster is realized.

A girl running across the fields, running towards where his machine will hit the earth. She is looking up at him, watching him crash, and he knows her as his daughter, come to greet him. And in this instant of realization, his experience of the world opens up to eternity, becomes infinite—there are no boundaries between himself and any other. He sees the girl watching him die and in the selfsame instant he is inside her head, running, running across the waves of leafy grass in the field, looking up at the sky. He sees the airplane as she sees it, her father's plane, with her father in it, in the instant before his death; and in his experience now of full eternity, his awareness is drawn back one step more from the girl to that of the watcher of this scene, seeing it all complete, in its full magnitude and detail, distilled by its greatness into a small, regressing window, a mirror, a television screen, an image of a girl in a field watching a plane crash with a man who is her father inside it, the watcher and the girl watching and the man in the plane watching the girl watching all as one. All of these fields of awareness are gathered together and held as one within his awareness, a glittering jewel he can hold and turn to see the light glance off its various facets. He can see it all from every perspective, he has opened himself to infinity. And as this leap of awareness overtakes him he realizes that there is another step back even from this, a watcher who is watching everything taking place here, everything he sees, even as he sees it, who sees everything that ever has been or will be, everything there ever is to see.

This instant of ultimate knowing sends him back, shunts the vision of the crashing airplane aside and brings him to a glistening tunnel of light. Does he suppose he could put a wall around infinity? There are no ends to where and when and what his full self can know. His complete being extends and expands in awareness beyond every earthly being, exuberant encompassing all glances backwards and forwards inward and outward up and around Glistering particles of light of every color streak past him surround his transparent conscious lightness of form, these particles seem to be the elemental particles of all matter—pure energy constantly in motion whirling twisting slamming together in one way and another to comprise whatever forms he may wish and in this forever instant they are implacable insensible insatiable in their fluctuating sprinkling of light across his vision indigo verdigris tarnish corrosion flush pure shadow net of gold pure white blue lightness looked intractable convincing his insensitivity angel came pulling following particles encircling that house and the censers of pure gold dull and faint in its magnificence sensible to dying discolored flashing flush across his visionary vision tarnish indecision all the sweet glad colours of the gardens of a dilated rough country house flashed and faded and formed of pure twisting particles of light At last he sees it all in its most pure form and instinct At last he knows how matter takes its shape—it is nothing more than light pulled together for a moment or two projected by his own image and imagining {protected by his own projection of his own imaging owned and owning only one can be here projecting and only the projector can project the image and watch what is projected} .light. stands still even as it flees him Wherefore ye shall make images of your emerods and images of your mice that mar the land peradventure he shall lighten his hand from off you particles that flee and flood his vision—clear for the sun changes oft for a blessing and a curse—which is a separation, between the light and the darkness; for he shall see the infinite in its entirety, the eternal in its breadth and its height and its length for space is time and time is space and both are light everlasting everchanging here and now; the particles which blaze their coursers past him begin to falter now begin to slow and dance—whichever ones he wanted are the ones he gathers unto himself and pours forth through himself and through his own vision he hears them now as sound solidified into frequencies variations of vibrations and tones, codified into curlicue alphabets streaming down and across his vision with the colors they apply and deny reaching through him with their meanings.

A piercing point of pure white light centered centrally in the center of his black field of vision sound awareness a silver star of flickering still white light—his focus is pure awareness locked upon it and for one moment it lingers its scintillating silver whiteness centered in his vision glimmering Therefore harken not to your prophets nor to your diviners nor to your dreamers the silver star grows bursts forth expands and pierces him to encompass all his vision all his sound and awareness all he ever is or was or will become home it is a vast white vastness a globe as wide as galaxies the Ancient of Ancients the Great Central Sun he floats above it in all its vastness, the Sun behind the Sun, the Source of all that exists Now and ever after he is one with All in All he is One with it and joined with it and all is One with him He sees deep into the interior of the Great Central Sun stares within its whiteness and sees glimpses of all that is SEES and IS mother resplendent father of myself behold this embryo of love and all wisdom his glory above the heavens three hundred and seventy thousand myriads of worlds lifted over flesh and strife blesséd above the fog of angles and fields of grain startled and huge in all its long face of glory emboldened to show forth all that is one with All in All; He is one with hunting silence care cruelty marble chorus possessed, one with lions eagles waltzes dances songs that whirl one with chains and pinions nails and screws and hammer blows, one with all that emits from the Great Central Sun, the Sun behind the sun, the star that fills his vision, he is one with all of it, all the explosions and catastrophes all the nights and glimpses ghastly dreams and wilderness wastes and garden fair One with cemeteries forest glen and harvest sowing yield and silent palette summit festivities dwelling-place of joy and despair Other planets other stars other than his own are emitted from this ONE all suns all systems all beings have one source the throne of the long face stands upon the firmament and has been before the beginning source of the short face of all creation by thirty-two paths the Ancient of Ancients extends to the uttermost of all creation even as a connection through a nerve from head to hip from mind to lip From the holy source everlasting emits the power that stirs the galaxies in their spiral whirling and all this He sees now and is one with it Flood forth from the source it can hold back no longer conceived brought forth unto Him and whether he received object climbed companion high and hastened enough death has loosed Him released Him this day taken from his midst flood forth and perplex Him in all its majesty perplexing myriad and glorious All that ever was and is and has been will be here now within the scope of his vision all emitting at once from the Great Central Sun all existing at once here conceived conspired and emitting All everything together all at once now plate blank clear venomous craft astounding vessels that sailed the vast space between the stars blank clear screen projection campfire of holographic shadow shapes projected observed by the projector problems come ensconced with their own solutions infants born wrapped in the day of their own demise Entertainments distractions distortions and deceptions cannot hide the source and solipsism of His being there is only One here common dust rainy summer shutting storybook armful spider crawling wonder

shiver up his spine amongst the bandages and terrible
sweetness of sex remote sensations trembling blessed
from the beginning and no end All food all seasons all
tremoring delicacies all warmness and light the cold of a
dripping block of ice numbers and all alphabets symbols
etchings engravings and handwritings scrawled across the
walls of all towns and cities and times never mind the
meanings they are all with him and within Him now Every
woman every man and all the children he has ever been
grown old and summarized in their lives and living
destroyed and grown ecstatic in the fullness of their being
the first dawn of every day is as stripped of introduction
and sweetness as the final time the sun will ever set they all
are here the same found out and realized and brought to
stillness and resumed Run longer faster fly higher exist to
exist be just to be it is only necessary to express the
infinitude encompassed in this single singularity brought
forth by means of holographic projection of waveforms
through the fabric of limitless energy He knows now and
is aware of all there is to be knowing how it is and came to
be he sees through the screen of all its glorious forms
inchained tomorrow the soul gusting forth constrained
within the statues and motion pictures of its aerial self-
created loving forms The various forms his Mind creates
and has created all laid out before him on a groaning
board these are all His creation and no two Creations are
alike His mind scans them all stationary held together as
one and all flying by the projection of his very own vision
bicycles variegated circles of his heart wars and aeons of

rust packed together loveliness and grief white iron and lead passed away shoulders legs and arms the soft curve of his lover's upraised thigh genitals and generals commanding thousands of boys to die if they existed or will exist his own eye envisioned them light-headed and comprised of light clean and full to the very last one reckoned through revelation and dead reckoning empyrean emormous plains and distances between the neutrons and protons in the nucleus of an atom those he hated and those he despised he created every ounce and full volume metric barbarous years and centuries of disbelief turmoil discord tumult and joy the sight of his daughter's eyes closed in sleep the touch of his fingertips on the thick hair at the back of his son's gorgeous head is enough to break him apart and pull him back together again Enumerate them try to grasp them as they stand still for a moment and fly by how can it be that everything is here now at once and all is ever changing They will all go as sure as they came and endeavored to enthrall Him they will all dissolve and dissipate into the bright white sunlight into the night his son his daughter his wife's sweet deliberate delight they are here and gone now they are as fleeting as school days puzzled morning fragrance riches ever-golden vanity conceit and the rest of the acts that are done and gone and given still though they come and go He is now one with All in All he is one with every vision every concept every discipline philosophy concordance every waking hour every dream All there is to be must come and go through HIM all is emitted through the

Central Sun through the reflected projection of his Being Everlasting one and all it is He is drawn back from within the great bursting glow and sees now that every person every object every conceivable conception table rock bridge and stone ocean wave and wall are glowing with the power of the source from whence they came All are emitted and transmitted through a screen of formalized ideals which are the thought forms of the highest Creation all receive their being from the projection of His thought constantly emitted and transmitted holographic transmission from within Come forth burst forth and break down the floodgates to flood forth from within the short face emits from the long face from the Ancient of Ancients from the highest holy one He sees himself in the glowing orb of every creature every beast and crawling insect every tree and leaf and burning shrub A life he once lived on a liquid planet orbiting the triple stars of Sirius one of the amphibious blue creatures swimming through the overheated oceans intelligent and cunning living one for another They are all burning with sacred fire they all pertain from inside turned without They are all governed by the lord of lords the law of all creation they are all mirrors of the one Keep going keep bringing forth for there never is an end to it Though He may turn away once more from his source he could never summon the courage the surfeit of power is never enough to stanch the flooding flow of wisdom which expresses him and sustains his expression, even in his disdain for his own creator do ye this in remembrance of me See each creature as his own creation flooded full of the glow of His own yearning and awareness He turns away from the myriad of myriads of worlds that pour forth from the ancient of ancients and sees his own small star his own blue world soaked in water salt of whiteness cloud and ocean He sees his focus spiked upon the village on that mountain that stone house he once and always for a brief moment called his own There upon the cold stone floor of their main living room a table is set, the wine glasses are filled, his own two children hand them from guest to guest. They are glowing… glowing, all of them surrounded and suffused in a sheath of golden stunning white light. His son and his daughter are glowing; the wine and the wine glasses they are handing to their neighbor Emmanuel from across the road, kind of him to come, these wine glasses are glowing. Emmanuel himself, an old Provençal man who has lived in the village and the farms nearby the village his entire life—Emmanuel is glowing. A species of golden white retrograde suffusion is emanating from his stooped-over back, the rolled up sleeves of his white dress shirt and every crooked work-wracked finger, tendon and limb of his ravaged used up body.

The table is glowing.

The walls and eaves and curious stone outcroppings of this two hundred and fifty year-old house are glowing. He sees it all from a vantage point high above, higher even than the point where he stands even now at the top of the stairs. The hair of their neighbor the shopkeeper Angelique from the main square of the village is glowing, as she accepts a glass of wine handed to her by his daughter—her hair and eyes and neck are all suffused with the tremendous full force of her being.

Then he sees her, his lovely Marya, covered in a garment of gold, suffused with glowing golden white light. She is filled with the holy oneness of all. She pauses on the stair, about to take the next step down towards the party. She pauses, as if remembering something she should bring with her, pauses and turns around.

Marya turns around.

And in this instant he sees her as she truly Is—she is a reflection of him. She is him and he is one with her. She is his reflection, a mirror of himself, an image of himself reflected back to him in glory. How could they have ever quarreled—any argument he ever had with her was an argument with himself. Any man, woman or child he ever killed, in those other lives, any man who hanged him or sacrificed him for the sake of a vengeful God, was himself slaughtering himself. He has been raised up high enough to know it. He can see it in her face, can see even now the wonder with which she sees him. He is the watcher now in her soul even as he is the watcher seeing himself at the top of the stairs, for he has become one with all in all. And he sees through her eyes the image of what he has become: a man but no longer a man in his body. His own form he sees, through her eyes, at the top of the stairs, the top of the mount, glowing radiant with golden white light, transfigured, his raiment white and glistering. He has been raised up and exalted, his consciousness ascended and expanded. She is his mirror and he is the image of the reflection of the one.

In glory he rises, his spirit restored to its rightful place amongst the highest heavens, amongst the clouds. No longer nailed to the body, his spirit has been set free. He can see, from this high summit above his restless wanderings upon the earth and amongst the stars, that vast corridor of his lives—that web of bright gems strewn across the broad expanse of space; both are timeless and endless, for they turn round and round upon themselves as a wheel does. Though his sins be as scarlet, they have been washed whiter than snow. Any life he once lived, any death he has suffered, any wayward indiscretion has been left behind him now—he is under grace, not under law. On the plane of eternity, every karmic debt is wiped away. There is no debt in the kingdom. He can hear voices echoing across the chasm of heavenly white light. Cascades assemble wind in the pillars of the clouds so he will make his holy name known, pure spirit of the watcher, the One who sees and knows, who calls forth and answers His own call. The Great Central Sun is calling him home. The lives he has lived will always be there if he wants them, for he IS God experiencing God as God. He is the seer and that which is seen. He is the singer and the listener and the notes of every song which has ever been sung.

Lifted up, raised above the stone house and the village perched on the tip of the mountain, he can see one last time the fluttering gossamer fabrics of that work of art he created when he was still Jacob, which he called *Entrevoir*, and though it will endure for only a brief instant in the vast expanse of the eternity of all time, he can see that it is an apt and beautiful expression of the nature of Spirit itself, ever flowing, ever changing even as it stands motionless at the peak of the mountaintop, reflecting through the eyes of the watcher the glorious light of the Sun.

## About the Author

Chris Katsaropoulos is the author of more than a dozen books, including three critically-acclaimed novels, *Fragile, Antiphony* and *Unilateral,* as well as *Complex Knowing,* the first collection of his poetry. He has been an editor at several major publishing houses and has published numerous trade books, textbooks, and novels over the course of his career. Chris enjoys traveling, playing the piano, and hiking in out of the way places. Visit antiphonyck.blogspot.com to read more, including his most recent poems.